Chris Ekral was born in South Wales and spent the first part of his life there, before his family moved to the East of England. The travel bug bit him and he spent time living, and working, in Japan and France, where *Survivor's Eyes* was largely written. He currently resides in London.

For Dave, Harry and Lilwen

Chris Ekral

SURVIVOR'S EYES

AUSTIN MACAULEY PUBLISHERS™
LONDON • CAMBRIDGE • NEW YORK • SHARJAH

Copyright © Chris Ekral 2023

The right of Chris Ekral to be identified as author of this work has been asserted by the author in accordance with sections 77 and 78 of the Copyright, Designs and Patents Act 1988.

All rights reserved. No part of this publication may be reproduced, stored in a retrieval system, or transmitted in any form or by any means, electronic, mechanical, photocopying, recording, or otherwise, without the prior permission of the publishers.

Any person who commits any unauthorised act in relation to this publication may be liable to criminal prosecution and civil claims for damages.

This is a work of fiction. Names, characters, businesses, places, events, locales, and incidents are either the products of the author's imagination or used in a fictitious manner. Any resemblance to actual persons, living or dead, or actual events is purely coincidental.

A CIP catalogue record for this title is available from the British Library.

ISBN 9781528997850 (Paperback)
ISBN 9781528997867 (ePub e-book)

www.austinmacauley.com

First Published 2023
Austin Macauley Publishers Ltd®
1 Canada Square
Canary Wharf
London
E14 5AA

I'd like to thank Jim for taking the time to read my draft and inspiring me to see the project through to completion. Equally, I could not have got this book done without the support and input of my mother, D, at every step of the way along my writing journey: thank you. Finally, I'd like to thank M, for always supporting me in everything I do and, above all, for her infinite reserves of patience!

Ship

The explosion woke me as it rattled the ship violently. I scrambled out of bed, deep below deck, shaking my head to try and clear it of sleep and confusion; how could anyone know I was there? I was always so careful, living by night with minimal lighting and heavy curtains and sleeping by day, safely hidden in the living quarters of the vessel.

If someone were to come aboard, they would think the ship empty, such was the level of caution I exercised. The only trace of my presence on the exterior was my fishing nets and even they were carefully draped around the hull so as to look like flotsam, as if they had drifted by chance into their current position, carried on the gentle waves that lapped the yellow sand of the nearby beach.

I clawed my way through the artificial darkness of my bedroom, reaching for a reassuring swig of the wine that was my only companion. I hurriedly thrust back the curtain covering the porthole and winced at the sudden intensity of the bright sunlight as I peered out with my naked eyes.

Once my enhanced vision had adjusted to both the glare and distance, I saw a large, black object whistle rapidly overhead, narrowly missing the main body of the vessel and landing with a huge impact just behind it, rocking the entire structure much more violently than before. It looked, bizarrely, like a cannonball, though I had never seen one in real life, only on film. There was a crumbling, colonial-era fort still standing on a hill, overlooking the harbour where the ship lay, and, judging by its direction and trajectory, I guessed that would be where the attack was coming from.

Sure enough, as I focused on the tower in the distance and gave my vision a brief second to adjust, I could make out a small group of people, near the ancient cannon that had once protected the bay from pirates and other aggressors. I did not need to look too closely, nor for too long, to conclude that they were not the kind of individuals I would ever want to become acquainted with.

If I'd had the time, I might have laughed at the irony of the fort's guns now being used by murderers and thieves (in other words, modern-day pirates) to attack me (representing, albeit loosely, civilisation). I might even have smiled at the twisted poetry of the situation, but time was not a luxury that I possessed, however, as a new cannonball arced high into the air and spurred me into sudden alert when it punched through the lookout post on the upper deck of my home. I lingered for a few brief seconds more, watching as the human detritus on the ridge staggered around, passing bottles of some no doubt vile liquor in a circle.

Three large, filthy men laughed and lashed out at each other, drunkenly, as they watched a smaller, scrawnier companion struggle to load the cannon from an ancient wooden barrel in front of the gun. He finished and walked unsteadily back to his jeering comrades, one of whom gave him a sudden and vicious blow to the face.

He crumpled to the ground but immediately got up, laughing inanely as he booted his aggressor hard in the groin. The larger man doubled over in pain for a split second before recovering enough to lash out with a powerful kick of his own. Scrawny danced out of the way of the blow but, in his inebriated state, could not maintain his balance and fell onto his backside whilst grinning stupidly at his mates, who clutched their sides in hilarity.

It was high-brow entertainment, to be sure, but as the smaller scumbag composed himself and staggered once more towards the cannon, I remembered that their sport was at the expense of my home and that I needed to get out of there quickly before I, too, became an incidental casualty of their afternoon's amusement.

My grandfather would always tell me to keep a bag packed 'just in case'. I used to think that was excessive, a result of growing up in a time when war was still a frequent threat. Since things went south, however, I followed his advice as a strict rule, and it always served me well. I whispered a quick 'thank you' to his departed soul as I grabbed my trusty backpack, which I had kept prepared since my arrival, from under the bed.

There was a knife, some food and a change of clothes inside, just the bare essentials necessary to survive, without any space for luxuries. Still, there was no time for self-pity, so I grabbed my pack and a jerrycan full of fresh rainwater, which I collected off the ship's deck during the frequent rainstorms, and sprinted down below to where my escape craft lay, ready and waiting for such a dark day as this.

Whilst I ran, the floor rumbled violently as yet another cannonball penetrated somewhere above my head with a huge crunch. Their aim was clearly improving, or possibly the alcohol was just starting to wear off.

The ship had, many years before, run aground on the jagged rocks that lined the sea floor along the coast and, thanks to their treachery, there was a large hole torn in the hull, which would serve as a perfect, and discreet, launch area for my escape vessel.

I looked a little suspiciously at the rowing boat rocking, almost nonchalantly, in the shallow water that had flooded the ship's interior. Boat was a grand word. It was more of a glorified coracle to be honest: a half-rotten, flimsy coracle. Though it had served me well on my desperate escape from the city the previous year, it had lain virtually unused for most of the time since and the gaudy, brown paintwork was visibly flaking in the sea air.

The exposed wood crumbled a little as I placed my hand on the boat's side to throw in my stuff, then swing my body in. It was most definitely not a pleasure vessel but, as long as it floated and held together long enough to make my escape, it was all I would need.

I grasped the oar firmly in one hand as I unhooked the tether from the rusting, salt-encrusted spike of metal that had held it in place. Then, taking the paddle in both hands, I pushed off from inside the hull and slipped out of the ship on the side facing away from the old fort and its cannon. I immediately proceeded to row as stealthily as possible, whilst also quickly putting distance between myself and the gun. I did not even pause to look back when another loud crash told me that the poor, ailing ship had taken a direct hit.

Keeping at a ninety-degree angle to the hull, I used the iron bulk of the vessel to hide me for as long as possible, before striking out across the open sea to my right, in the direction of a small estuary I sometimes visited. At that point, I hoped that the glare of the midday sun directly behind me, reflecting off both the water and the remaining paint on my boat, would shield me well-enough from any eyes that might stray my way.

My destination was a tiny forest, situated where a small river met the sea in a miniature tidal delta. The fishing was good there and the view inspirational. I had often lingered in that place of an evening, high in a tree, and gazed longingly out across the ocean, my soul aching for the home I knew I would never see again and which probably, in all likelihood, no longer existed.

In all honesty, I did not even know which direction home lay in, but the mind quickly turned to such melancholic musings when alone, nursing a bottle of wine, and to wallow in bittersweet reminiscing rarely needed any more than the slightest of encouragements. Thus, in a strange way, I had always thought of that tiny patch of greenery as a special place. That day, however, it would be my sanctuary, somewhere to lie low while I decided on my next move.

The sand suddenly crunched beneath me and I jumped into the water to pull the boat ashore, covering it urgently with reeds and seaweed to hide my tracks before I climbed the nearest tree. That gave me a great vantage point from where to observe the unfolding tragedy, which I had just so narrowly managed to escape.

Clearly, the ship had broken its back on the reef many, many years ago. It had outlived its usefulness long before the virus struck and had been abandoned by all as a lost cause. Despite this, it had persisted, against all expectations, enduring even the end of the very civilisation that had built it. Eventually, it had provided a refuge for me, a solitary man fleeing the death throes of a culture that he had never felt a part of, never cared for. A man who now mourned that bygone age, as keenly as the loved ones whose bones probably decorated the ground, somewhere in a far-off land.

The ship, like a prize-fighter who refused to be knocked out, could not sink, but this stubborn valour served only to prolong its agony as it was gradually pounded into nothing by the cannon fire, for no other reason than to briefly entertain a few mindless scumbags.

To destroy what others had made, to slaughter and rape those they did not know and to steal what they wanted, that was life for people such as those firing the cannon. They lived like animals, revelling in their atrocities, with no empathy or motive beyond their own immediate gratification. Truly, they exemplified what had become of us, the human race.

I watched, tears stinging my eyes, as their aim improved, and each further direct hit caused the boat to collapse in on itself a little more. Although I felt a deep sense of personal sorrow, I could also see a much bigger, symbolic picture.

To my weary eyes, the ship was a proud monument to the heights reached by the society that created it, which had now vanished. More poetically, I imagined it as a metaphor for civilisation itself. Nature had dealt it a cruel hand and it had foundered on the rocks, a hair's breadth from the chasm of destruction. Amazingly, it had survived, battered and broken, but still extant, notwithstanding the odds. Yet, despite this miracle, it found itself defenceless against the mindless brutality of those who dreamed only of destruction.

The metaphor, though arguably tenuous, was powerful and what was nothing more than a minor drama became, in my mind, something that resonated much more deeply, much more tragically. I screwed my eyes shut against the sight of the ship burning fiercely as some remaining fuel deep in the hold ignited. A single, futile tear escaped my left eye and trickled down my face, then off my chin, running briefly along the sand in a valiant, but ultimately doomed, attempt to join with the vast expanse of salt water that filled the estuary around me.

I sat still, watching, for a long, long time, until the fire now leaping relentlessly from within the hold completely smothered the vessel in its withering embrace. I imagined the shouts and cries of satisfaction from the scumbags manning the guns, as the last of the ship's burnt remains folded meekly into the sea.

At last, I decided to leave. I could still smell the smoke on the evening breeze as I retrieved my rowboat and, without looking back, pushed off to head upriver in search of a new place to live, somewhere else to scrape an existence out of a savage new world.

Bag

I stood there, stock-still, enticed by its shine like a magpie eyeing up an empty bottle. Seconds before, I had been preparing to head home when *something* had caught my eye.

I was on one of my semi-regular trips to one of the small towns in the area, of which there were many. More accurately, the place had once been a town but now it was nothing more than a skeletal shell of its former incarnation, picked clean by scavengers and grinning vacantly, bleached and stark, at the sun.

I had never been to this particular collection of ruins before, but others certainly had; it was barren and had long-since been looted of anything I might have deemed useful. That was hardly unusual, most former settlements in the area were thus. Indeed, I would not have been surprised at all if the rest of the world were stripped-bare, too. Still, I came to such places on an endless quest for something to break up the monotony. I never knew what I might find and there was always something hidden away, somewhere the scumbags would not have the intelligence to look. At any rate, it was infinitely preferable to catching fish.

The town had obviously been ransacked many times over and bore the scars to prove it: shattered windows, smoke-stained walls and large, frequent patches of dried blood. I had, nevertheless, found a few cans of food, including a tin of peaches in syrup, and, even better, a few bottles of local wine to nurse me through those bleak winter nights or help me while away the long, lonely summer evenings.

The place would once have had a name, but I had never bothered to find it out and such a thing was now irrelevant, an anachronism. To know its location was quite enough for me. I finally understood the completely arbitrary nature of naming places, of naming a person. They were merely verbal tags by which something could be identified, or a concept talked about. With nobody to talk to, no one to communicate with, names had lost all significance.

Even my own seemed to be receding from my memory, becoming more and more difficult to recall, as I never had any need of it. My most recent human contact had begun with a surprised shout, swiftly progressing to become an attempted murder, which was immediately followed by a successful murder, though I would, naturally, plead self-defence. This seemed to be what 'society' had become and what, for its foreseeable future, it would be.

The nameless town had very little left to offer anyone, except perhaps a stark attestation of how much we had lost, a savage testament to how quick our regression had been. To illustrate this, the remains of unfortunate people could be found, strewn at depressingly regular intervals around the streets of the forgotten settlement, in doorways, on stairwells: lying where they fell, their bones picked clean by animals and cracked in the unrelenting sun.

These were not victims of disease. *They* had, mostly, been buried in mass pits outside and upwind of settlements. The virus had claimed many, many lives and it killed horrifically, with mucus bubbling and blood streaming from orifices as lungs liquefied and ribs collapsed. It did not, however, leave knife marks or bullet holes on skeletons, still wracked with their owner's last dying agony. It did not leave corpses of women lying with torn clothes and bloodied, exposed bodies by the side of the road and it did not leave small cadavers in huddled heaps, emaciated and rotting, as they waited in vain for a slaughtered parent to return with food or medicine. The virus did not do all this. We did.

By a cruel twist of fate, the unfortunates littering the town had been survivors. They had avoided the virus, beating improbable odds only to later die a brutal death at the hands of their own species. There was probably some bittersweet irony in that, but I'd seen way too much in recent years for that to even begin to move me.

Countless stories, films and theories in our more civilised days told of how a crisis would unite humanity in the face of adversity or a threat to its existence. Historians pointed to examples in our past of warring tribes joining forces in the face of an external danger: the city states of Ancient Greece, or the Medieval Crusades, but when the virus struck, none but a pitiful few had any noble intentions regarding the human race and its continuation.

When it came to crunch time, most cared for nothing beyond their own immediate survival. I suppose it is easy to be objective and altruistic when you have a full stomach and a roof over your head but take that away and our true animal core is revealed: kill for gain and steal to survive. Those who stuck rigidly to civilised conduct quickly became food for the rats, or worse. Everyone else either surrendered to base instinct or was reluctantly forced to become a killer in order to survive. I knew which of those groups I belonged to; anyone still alive had lost at least a little of that which made us human and I was no exception.

Lost in such thoughts, I slunk along in the lengthening shadows, though the place seemed devoid of any apparent danger, so no need for excessive caution. I glanced idly around me as I walked and my wandering eyes came to rest upon the gutted remains of what must have been an unusually large house, set back slightly from the road.

Every single building in the ravaged town bore fire scars, or so it seemed, but this one was considerably more sizeable than any other dwelling that I had seen there and, as a result, my gaze lingered on it, my curiosity piqued. As I stared, the sun appeared from behind a cloud and I saw a strange glint suddenly dance from the shadows of the overgrown front garden. With nothing better to do, I headed towards it, very much intrigued.

When I nonchalantly pushed the rusted gates open, they gave a hideous screech as long-neglected hinges ground against one another in violent protest. I dropped to the ground instantly, cursing myself for my lapse in concentration. Although the town appeared deserted, you could never really know for sure and announcing your presence so obviously was never anything but foolish.

After a few long and tense minutes, lying concealed from view in the thick shelter of what was, undoubtedly, once a neatly trimmed and well-maintained hedge, I rose cautiously to my feet and entered the front garden. Suitably chastened, I did not close the gate behind me, in order to avoid making any more unnecessary noise.

I softly approached the source of the light and was not even remotely surprised to find a virtually complete male skeleton poking up out of the lush grass, vegetation probing through the bones and colonising the tattered remnants of its business wear. It was not that, however, that had caught my eye: human remains were hardly rare. Rather, it was what was clutched, still tightly, between the fingers of the dead man's left hand that had brought me there, to his final resting place.

It was some kind of bag, more a briefcase which, given its long exposure to the elements, seemed remarkably intact; its gold buckles still bright and untarnished. That only served to add further fuel to my curiosity, so I bent to retrieve it from where it lay under its former owner's ribs, which were still protecting his property in calcified defiance.

As my hands closed around the handle, I paused for a brief second to examine the scene as it must have played out. Judging by the weathered nature of the bones and their being semi-embedded in the ground, I concluded that he had met his end at least a year ago, probably more, around about the time society was spasming in its final death throes and all order had finally broken down.

The man's body lay directly beneath a large, second floor window. He had obviously jumped, but it didn't look like the fall had killed him. The skeleton was hunched, deliberately, over the briefcase, as if seeking to protect it with his body, even as he lay injured and prone.

The back of his skull, facing away from the soil, had been completely caved in with what looked to be a couple of heavy, deliberate blows with a blunt instrument. Upon closer examination, I could see that his teeth were imbedded in the outer material of the bag due to the force of the attack. The strokes appeared effectively administered and neat; the killer, or killers, obviously knew exactly what they were doing.

There were no clues as to who his murderers were, but it could have been anyone. Previously mild-mannered suburbanites had risen to the brutal challenge of this savage new world with alarming alacrity; care workers became robbers; nurses became rapists and teachers became child killers. With a sudden stab of remorse, I looked at my own hands and could almost see the blood staining them; it was getting harder and harder to convince myself that I was one of the good guys.

What was intriguing, however, was why the killer, or killers, hadn't taken the case. Evidently, the owner considered what was in there worthy of dying for but there must have been something else of value that they were after.

Perhaps the man had food, medicines or even a female companion, I mused. I would never know for sure, of course, but I did know that the definition of 'valuable' had changed significantly in such dark days.

Lifting my gaze from the bones, I studied the house itself. The front door of the mansion had been kicked in and the place set alight, judging by the large pyre of combustibles in the hallway. This was obviously done to smoke out the occupants, and it appeared to have been successful, judging by the leap that the briefcase owner had taken. I briefly thought about venturing into the house but quickly decided against it. More than likely, I would not like what I found and, although my eyes were no longer strangers to slaughter and death, the horrors never got any easier to see. Even atrocities I'd witnessed long ago still stung the spirit, haunting me deeply.

I gently pulled the dead man's fingers away from the case and laid his hands softly on the ground next to his head. I then hurriedly sanitised my own hands, with a bottle from my backpack, to rid them of any traces of the virus that could be present in the remains; it survived far longer on organic bodies than it did on objects. Once that was done, I carefully prised the case away from under the skull, taking care to respectfully lower the ravaged cranium onto the ground and setting the bag to rest against my knee. Perhaps unsurprisingly, it was locked shut and, despite much shaking and squeezing of the mechanism, it would not immediately yield up its secrets.

I knew then that I had to take it with me, although it would definitely encumber me on my bike. To be brutally honest, I really did not have very much excitement in my life at all, so leaving it behind was not an option I was willing to consider.

As I stood up with the case in my grip, I could not shake the nagging feeling that my actions were somewhat irreverent: akin to desecrating a burial site. I decided that I must do something to show respect, to convince myself that I was different, a better person than his murderers, but I had nothing with which to dig a grave, nor the time to make one. Instead, I made my way across to an overgrown flower bed, collected a few armfuls of bright blossoms and laid them slowly on top of the man's body, taking care not to touch it and kneeling solemnly on the grass as I did so.

It seemed a woefully inadequate gesture, but I at least felt that I'd returned a little of the dignity that had been so cruelly smashed out of him and, more pertinently, had somehow retained a fraction of my own. A simple act, maybe, but symbolic of something deeper, something beyond the stark profanity of the scene before me.

Tearing my eyes from the bones, I clutched the briefcase to my chest and glanced up at the ever-beautiful sun, setting majestically in a sky of glorious red and gold swathes. I briefly pondered, as I often did, on how strange it was that the stars and our planet were essentially the same as before, yet our existence had changed so completely.

We had thought that the world was ending, but it was only the end of *our* world, a world entirely of our creation. Faced with this stark realisation, it was impossible to deny how fragile and artificial it had actually been in the first place. Nature cared little for morality, whether we were promoted, what kind of car we drove or what ethnicity we were. Our society, a glorious testament to our superiority as a species, was gone, but the world carried on regardless.

I saw birds wheeling across the sky, heard insects beginning to find their voices as the evening deepened towards night and felt the gentle breeze tugging at my hair, all as it always had been. I stood in the ruins of the town as an anomaly, representing something that had ceased to exist, even as I was surrounded by the perfect continuity of the natural world.

Much had been written about the need for us, as a species, to live in a manner more akin to nature, as our 'savage' ancestors had. Romanticism dictated that we should look to the past for a better way to live, a way to live in harmony with the planet.

This was fine as a theory, but it conveniently glossed over the true nature of our forebears: homicidal, superstitious brutes who murdered strangers and feared or worshipped that which they did not understand. Ancient Rome had centrally heated houses and high levels of social organisation, but they brutally tortured their enemies and slaughtered those who resisted 'enlightenment' at their hands. One had only to look to the animal kingdom to see that the natural way was kill-or-be-killed; domination of the weak by the physically strong; inflicting pain and suffering on others to ensure one's own survival. We were well and truly back in the murderous arms of Mother Nature.

I remained kneeling, lost in reflection, for a long while, fighting the urge to crack open one of the bottles in my swag bag to keep me company, but night was fast approaching. It would soon be time to go; I always travelled in darkness when venturing somewhere unknown or further afield.

The reason for this was clear: the scumbags that I might encounter by daylight, lying in wait along the roads for any hapless passing traveller, would not be present. They usually would have abandoned their 'work' for the evening and would be doing whatever it was they did in their free time, raping, murdering and drinking, probably.

In the unlikely event that there were an encounter, it was also infinitely easier to escape in the dark. The obvious downside was that night travel sometimes meant slow or even painful progress, although if it came to a choice between scraped knees or being tortured and killed, I would not hesitate to choose the former, but call me old fashioned.

Thinking practically, I still had a long, long way to go in the dark, on a bicycle, so being drunk would not help in any way at all. With a sterling effort of will, I resisted the siren-call emanating from the depths of my backpack and merely sat there on the overgrown lawn, with the skeleton, holding the case in my hand and pondering on my, and our, changed existence while waiting for the darkness to completely conquer the sun's resistance.

At last, when I could no longer see my hand clearly in front of my face, I decided it was time to go. Avoiding the treacherous gate, I pushed gently through the bushes as silently as possible, conscious that noise travelled much further in the still of the night than it did in the daytime hours, or it certainly seemed to. I could not ignore the possibility that the place had nocturnal denizens, who might find courage in the dark that they lacked in broad daylight and make a play.

I moved stealthily, making barely a sound as I padded along the main street of the town. This speedy discretion was a recently acquired skill, one that I had developed since trusting strangers to be good natured had become a potentially fatal character flaw.

I halted immediately as a pair of glowing red orbs detached themselves from the shadows and moved towards me. The eyes suddenly stopped dead and fixed on my position. I first saw that it was a fox and then I smelt it; their odour had not improved an iota, even with the absence of human society and its associated refuse. I reached blindly for the knife in the back of my waistband and advanced slowly towards the creature: fox was not exactly the tastiest of meats, but it would be a welcome break from fish. Just as I approached to almost within striking range, however, the wind changed direction and the creature fled as it caught my scent advancing. I cursed under my breath and sheathed my knife.

I slipped once more down the pitch-black street, heading towards the edge of town where my battered bicycle lay, carefully concealed in a patch of thick undergrowth.

There were no lights visible in any of the windows that gave onto the street. That reassured me, to a certain extent, that the town was empty, or at least empty of anyone who might pose a threat. Nobody in their right mind would want to advertise their presence with a bright light at night-time and anyone stupid enough to do so would not have survived so long.

A lit window could only mean one of two things: a trap or that the occupants did not fear an attack. They might be armed with guns or possess strength in numbers, maybe both. That would certainly make them people to fear and avoid, but luckily, I saw nothing to suggest any such danger. If, despite all appearances, there were someone there and they spotted me roaming the streets like a vampire of old-time myth, then all the signs indicated that they would choose discretion over aggression, and that was fine by me.

I reached my bike's hiding place without incident, navigating more by sense than sight. It always amazed me just how dark it was now that electricity no longer illuminated the night sky. I had lived in the city my whole life, previously, and had never known true darkness: there was always a street or shop light to brighten even the bleakest winter night, but there, I could barely see my feet beneath me. Perhaps, in another life, I would have been afraid of such blinding gloom, but I had long since learned that the only thing I needed to fear on this earth was my fellow human.

As quietly as possible, I pulled my bicycle out of the bushes, picking a few lingering twigs and leaves out of the spokes as I checked the tyres. The bike was one of the few things I had stolen back in the early days of our end and it had served me extremely well.

I had prided myself on not looting back in the city, but I'd needed transport when I reached the coast, after fleeing the ship, and realised that my battered old boat would never get me anywhere upstream.

I had seen a few bicycles in a cracked shop window, but the owner was still there, defending his store with a gun. I tried to reason with him, explaining that the world order had changed, offering him food and water in exchange for a bike but he was too stubborn, or stupid, to understand. Eventually, I broke in while he was sleeping and took the best bike he had, leaving some food as an apology. While the rest of humanity was slaughtering each other for cars and fuel, I would travel easily and silently through their midst on my metal steed, as they slept.

The bulk of the briefcase meant that I'd have to travel more slowly than usual, but, anyway, I was in no real rush to get back to the riverside shack that I called home. There was nothing and nobody waiting for me there, just an illusion of security: I kept the surrounding area as clear of scumbags as possible and the vicinity was uninviting for anyone lacking the nous to survive in the wilderness. Still, death in this savage new world was only ever a mere slice of bad luck away.

While it could never be said that my home was a palace, it allowed me to survive in splendid isolation and even, occasionally, fool myself into believing that I was some kind of noble in a savage world, or at the very least a noble savage. Most of the time, though, I just felt cripplingly lonely, and there was nothing very heroic about that, though the wine certainly helped hold at bay such feelings, even if it could not completely suppress them.

The two-hour ride back passed without incident; I might even say that I enjoyed it. I saw no living soul nor animal upon my solitary, silent journey and that was just the way I liked it. What's more, the briefcase that I held balanced across the handlebars was not as encumbering as I had feared. Even so, I was glad to see the moonlight reflected back at me, rippling on the surface of the water, telling me that I was home.

The river was the only friend I had in the world. It fed, hydrated and kept me safe from one direction at least. Coming to a stop, I gently lifted the heavy foliage, carefully arranged to look natural, which concealed the waterproofed pit that I used to store my bicycle, safe from the elements. I heaved my trusty steed in then covered it up, as I lowered the disguise once more over its location and prepared to enter my sanctuary.

My home was built as a hidden enclosure on all sides, with the open riverbank to the front. I had constructed it using pieces of scavenged wood and plastic, which I used to cover the spacious pit dug into the ground beneath, and then topped the low-lying structure with ferns and other foliage as a natural roof, which was mostly waterproof.

I had planted cuttings and diligently watered and coaxed them into life, so that they now covered my home with a living shield of disguise. I had also painstakingly transplanted a hedge around my immediate living space, and it had sprouted to a suitable height and thickness to stop anyone seeing in. I did not trim it, of course; it grew wild. This was to give the impression of the overgrown remnants of a garden. If anyone peeked through the hedge, all they would see was an unassuming mound of foliage and nothing of immediate interest. It was this meticulous caution, and attention to detail, which enabled me to live under the illusion of apparent safety.

My feeling of security stemmed only from the power of absolute discretion. It had to appear that there was nobody, and nothing of value, there. I had installed rudimentary but effective soundproofing, using salvaged cardboard and polystyrene to deaden any sound which I might emit, though I seldom made much noise anyway. I had a guitar that I'd found somewhere, but I only picked it up rarely, when the silence got too much. Usually, there seemed little point in playing when there was no one to listen.

My greatest feat of engineering was a hidden chimney, which used vents dug into the soft earth to draw any smoke from a fire away, and out, through a number of dispersed pits fifty metres away. It had taken a lot of work and did not function perfectly: my clothes smelt permanently of burnt wood in the colder months, but it would draw any inquisitive prowlers away from my home. The ventilation holes were surrounded by leaves to disguise their true function, with the idea being that any chance observer would dismiss the smoke as natural, rising from the damp ground.

All in all, I was as safe as I could be in that savage wilderness, provided no one stumbled upon my location by chance; even the most cautious survivor could be undone by nothing more than a little bad luck or poor timing.

After hiding my bike and grabbing a big bundle of wood for the fire, I entered my home through its concealed trapdoor and shut myself in for the night, taking the briefcase and my spoils from the day with me. I immediately opened one of the bottles of wine that I had found, pouring it into the solitary, cracked glass that I possessed whilst thinking it was perhaps time to upgrade my crystalware. I then spent fifteen minutes lighting and stacking the fire precisely, so as to provide enough warmth but not too much smoke. Finally, I sat down and forensically examined the briefcase I had carried back with me.

It was made of plush leather, though faded, obviously, but would once have been very expensive. I picked it up and shook it but could hear nothing from within. Once again, I noticed how surprisingly light it was. I tried another time to force the lock, but there seemed to be no way to access the contents without destroying it, so I delayed my next move for a while as I allowed myself to ponder upon what it contained.

This was the most exciting thing to happen in my life for a long, long while and I did not want the thrill to be over too soon. Maybe, I thought excitedly, it contained some kind of jewels or artwork that the scumbags would not recognise or understand.

I allowed my mind to wander into the realms of the fantastical and the far-fetched for a short while, my imagination piqued and fuelled by wine and the warmth of the fire soothing my aching body, filling me with a deep glow of temporary contentment. Finally, though, I grew bored of merely hypothesising and resolved to make the bag yield up its secrets.

I took a long, sharp knife, which I usually used for skinning fish, from the hook where it hung and contemplated the task of accessing the case's contents. I had no wish to break or blunt the blade by attempting to pick the extensive and intricate lock system. Instead, I thrust the knife into the age-weakened leather panelling that made up the case's structure.

With a bit of effort, I managed to cut through the tough material and prise off one of the side panels, only to be greeted with a large, opaque plastic bag, completely filling the interior; no wonder it had not rattled when I shook it. I felt through the polymer but all I could deduce was that it contained something hard and flat, so I extricated the bag entirely from the gaping case and laid it carefully on the floor.

It was a plain, non-descript plastic carrier, such as one would have received in any shop of the old society. Gone now was my desire to draw out the entertainment; I had to know what was in the bag more than anything else in the world. I opened it and peered in, but it was too dark to make anything out in the dim and flickering light that the small fire provided.

I reached in and attempted to grab the contents but I was puzzled to instead find myself holding something paper-like, yet rather brittle. I pulled my hand out of the bag and towards the light of the fire.

To my surprise, I was holding a wad of cash, neatly stacked and bound together with a currency marker from an old bank. That was the last thing I had been expecting and, for a while, I just stared, dumbfounded. I eventually regained my senses and emptied the rest of the contents onto the floor.

I examined my haul: all banknotes. I had not seen money of any variety for a long, long time, and certainly nothing more than a few old coins, lying discarded. The notes were still clean and crisp, as if they had freshly come from a cash dispenser and the bright colours were only slightly faded and mildewed from their long neglect.

I looked at that pile of currency and residual instinct kicked in, instantly compelling me to see how much money was there. In a display of pure capitalist programming, I grabbed each stack of notes and counted it carefully, yet feverishly.

When at last I was done, I sat back and processed the figure. It was a fortune, the kind most people used only to dream of, the sort of bank balance that centuries of advertising and media had convinced us was the be-all and end-all, the meaning of life and guaranteed happiness. I too, despite my antipathy and loathing of society at large, had fantasised about such wealth and the freedom it would entail. Now, in a cruel mockery of fate, it was mine.

I poured another glass of wine as I allowed myself to drift off into drunken musing, dreaming of everything that the money laid out before me could once have provided. In my mind, I bought fast cars, enjoyed the company of beautiful people, wore designer clothes and did designer drugs whilst drinking the finest champagne from cut-crystal glasses. I owned a penthouse apartment in the city overlooking the river, a sprawling mansion in the country, everything I had ever been conditioned to believe that I truly wanted.

Sadly, we had not seen the potential for tragedy inherent in billions of people sharing the same, manufactured, material aspirations. We had not been wise enough to recognise the seeds of our own doom being planted in our heads and sown amongst us. Still, I allowed myself to linger, drunkenly, in my reverie, escaping my brutal reality by revisiting the anachronistic dreams of the man I used to be.

After a long moment, in which I achieved everything I used to desire that no longer existed, I sat, holding a handful of cash, and gazed at the faded embers of the fire that had slowly died during my idle musing.

The night had begun to set in, and I could feel the chill starting to seep into the corners of the room, where the warmth of the fire no longer reached. A quick glance at my woodpile told me that I had enough logs to last me comfortably through the night, but no kindling to get the flames going again. I really didn't fancy stepping outside, half-drunk, into the cold, unwelcoming dark.

I glanced around my home for anything I could use instead but there was nothing immediately apparent, apart from…

I hesitated for a few long seconds, thinking of the poor bastard with his brains bashed in on his front lawn but, eventually, I grabbed a few wads of banknotes, untied them and threw them on the embers, arranging a night's worth of logs on top.

Leaning back on my haunches, I blew until I coaxed a small tongue of flame beneath, and then inside, the kindling. I watched a while as the flames grew larger, their withering beauty spreading inexorably across famous faces, long dead and stripped of all significance. Finally, I sat back in my favourite place before the hearth, reached for another glass of wine and settled down for the rest of the evening.

Wine

'If all else fails, we can always drink wine'. I had once seen that daubed on a train window, many years ago, and had laughed at the sentiment, thought it was quaint. I laughed no longer as the truth of those words hit home every single day.

I was utterly alone, living in a filthy hovel by a forgotten river. I shunned the very few people that I came into contact with. Now that the virus had run its course, my greatest fear was my fellow men, what they had become and what I had had to become as a result. In the absence of any hope, one found solace in what one could and mine rested firmly within the bottle before me, the bottles chilling in the river outside and the bottles yet to be 'rescued'.

To call the drink before me a vintage would be nothing but an anachronism. All the wine that was still in existence was now, by default, vintage, as there were no longer any vineyards to make any more.

Think, if you would, on the social structure required to produce the bottle from which I was drinking. It would take organisation on a huge scale and a large number of people working together, for a common goal, in order to cultivate and nurture the vines. To harvest the grapes and produce wine from them would involve cooperation on a wide level, the use of advanced technology and good, old-fashioned hard work.

These were all concepts that we took for granted in the past, but they had become completely redundant. Why work when you could just steal the fruits of someone else's labour? Why produce when you could just consume and destroy?

It also took trust to make wine, trust that no one would steal the grapes off your vines and faith that you would not merely be inviting an early, and brutal, death at the hands of those who coveted what was not theirs and would seek to take it by force. I hid myself away from all prying eyes because I had no such faith and did not want to announce my presence by cultivating the land so obviously, even for vegetables.

I chose to live off what the forest and river provided, and to scavenge the rest. Not exactly the choice of a philanthropist, nor that of Achilles, but faith in humanity was a virtue in extremely limited supply in this savage new world. It was also a virtue which would, most probably, get you killed.

The absence of any semblance of trust between contemporary people rendered any attempt at social organisation impossible so, as a result, the production of wine was also now impossible. It was a product of a by-gone age, so simple and yet symbolic of how far, and how quickly, we had fallen. More pertinently, however, it begged the question: what to do when the wine failed?

I did not think I would be able to cope. The will to live is strong in all life forms but I was only just about surviving by drinking wine, to numb the feelings of crushing hopelessness and creeping horror.

I had tried before to make cider from the plentiful apples around the area. I scavenged yeast and sugar and eventually succeeded in making something alcoholic that was drinkable, but it was never a patch on what was in the bottle before me. It did the job of anaesthetising me for a few hours, but I certainly wouldn't offer a cup to a guest, if I ever had such a thing.

I had only ever been a consumer of wine, never a producer and the skills to make it had probably died with its manufacturers. So much knowledge had been lost with our society's demise; millennia's worth of accumulated wisdom had simply disappeared when the power grid went down, taking computer systems with it. Some would still exist in books, but that was only in the cities and God only knew what horrors now dwelt there.

Anything I did not myself know was forever beyond my reach and the human race was only able to operate with the skills its remaining individuals possessed. I had seen many a corpse lying, obviously murdered, in the empty drinks section of a looted supermarket, and I knew exactly why: we might no longer possess the know-how, but we'd gladly kill for its fruits.

Consequently, all I did was sit, night after night, deep in my oblivion, nursing a bottle of wine and drinking from an exquisite cut-glass goblet, which I had found a while back in the remnants of a grand hotel overlooking the river. Though there had been many, many glasses there, I had taken only one: I did not need two. There was also a real fear that having a set of two glasses would open up a clear path to memories that were too acutely painful to bear: memories of a friend, memories of shame and regret at my impotence in the face of events beyond the scale of my control.

Such thoughts might also awaken something within me that had lain dormant for so long. Desires that needed little to trigger. Desires that gnawed constantly at the edge of sanity and screamed loudly in the vacuum of solitude. I remembered well how difficult it always was to pacify such impulses once aroused, and I feared I would not be able to do so. As a result, I only possessed one glass.

Wresting my mind from the darkness deep within the psyche, ever straining at its constraints, I looked briefly out of my trapdoor at the sun setting slowly over the rippling water. My heart ached to see such beauty still in the world, although I knew, deep down, that it could only ever be a bittersweet respite from the pain of existence.

I stared mournfully at the bottle in my hands as I poured a fresh glass to raise a toast to the setting sun. Wine used to have such romantic connotations: it was civilised, cultured and refined, but sadly, all it had become was a means for me to forget my miserable existence, for a few hours at a time.

I used to enjoy drinking wine, now I merely used it. The scumbags drank it and so did I, for exactly the same reason. We had dragged this once-elegant concept down, with ourselves, to our current pitiful trough of existence. As I sipped, I held the half-empty bottle in my other hand and all I could think was what a shame it would be to throw it away, since it would make such a handy weapon.

The regression was complete.

Persistence

The first time I saw her, I could scarcely believe my eyes: a *real* woman. She seemed to be alone, too. I could not remember the last time I'd seen anyone, let alone a female, of my species and in my excitement, my usual caution failed me for a brief, crazy moment.

I ran towards her, waving my arms and shouting a greeting. She turned and stood still, immobilised with shock, staring at me for a split second, before she drew an arrow back in the bow that I had failed to notice in my elated state.

"I'm friendly!" I shouted, as I stopped running and threw my hands up in the air in a gesture of surrender. She hesitated for a brief moment before letting the arrow fly. It shot towards me at an alarming speed, and I had to throw myself sideways to avoid it embedding itself squarely in my chest.

I hit the ground hard, taking a mouthful of earth for my troubles, but I immediately sat up, spitting soil and wiping my mouth on a sleeve as I cursed under my breath. The impact had brought me to my senses and reminded me of the need for extreme caution, at all times.

Despite the close call, I was still determined to make contact with her, but I now knew that I would need to take my time and attempt to gain her trust. I got to my feet gingerly, brushing dried mud and twigs out of my beard and hair. Looking around furtively, I could see no sign of my assailant, so I started off after her in the direction she had been heading, hoping to trail her, wherever she was going.

I had learned to read the woods fairly well over my years spent in solitude by the river, not bad for a former city-dweller, so following a fleeing human was no trouble at all.

I could hear her moving through the undergrowth ahead of me, but I made no attempt to catch her up. She probably thought she was moving quietly and that I would not be able to follow her, so I did nothing to suggest otherwise. I just hung back, keeping my distance but also keeping her within earshot.

I had the sudden brainwave that I could follow her home, find out where she lived and then attempt to make contact, much more tactfully than the recent, near-fatal first encounter, of course. In truth, I was desperate for a human connection. I had lived far too long alone and it was killing me, slowly but surely. To spend too long in complete solitude eats away gradually at the hope that is an essential part of living. Without hope, one is merely surviving, staving off one's inevitable end for as long as possible, with no ulterior goal.

All of a sudden, the tracks came to an abrupt stop, and I crouched instinctively down on all fours. At first, I could see nothing against the uniform green and brown background, then she moved, ever so slightly, and I picked her out. She was standing completely still against the trees, listening and watching, her head moving almost imperceptibly left and right, scanning the area.

I crawled closer, painfully slowly, to get a better view of her. She was slim, though no one I ever saw was overweight those days. She was not, if I were to be honest, classically attractive, but she had certain 'qualities' that I, as a man, lacked and I found her immediately, incredibly alluring. As for my own appearance, I hadn't looked in a mirror for years but a quick, self-conscious feel of my straggly beard and a look at my filthy hands told me that neither was I, myself, a work of art.

She stood, watching without seeing, while I lay, watching her without being seen, for around five minutes before she gracefully disappeared into a hole in the ground that she then covered with a ready-stitched carpet of foliage.

I stood still for a few minutes, taking stock of my location and mentally retracing my steps that morning. I knew exactly how I had got there and where I was in relation to my home, but that area of the woods was unfamiliar, and I desperately wanted to be able to find my way back to see her again.

I was very confident in my navigational ability and that I would be able to return, despite not having been there before. Nonetheless, I broke a few branches off as I made my way back, to mark my route, just in case. I thought how fortunate it was that, happily, a whim had brought me this way for a change, a mere ten minutes from my own hole in the ground but a little further inland.

I had never previously explored the area as I had determined it too far from the river to harbour any decent food sources and, therefore, not worth the effort. That morning, however, I had been feeling especially restless and had decided to go somewhere off my beaten track, in search of a break from the crushing monotony of existence. I idly wondered how long we had been neighbours, without knowing, and almost kicked myself for my criminal lack of adventure. I determined then and there to come back, as soon as possible.

***

As she emerged from her home early the next morning, I sat perfectly still and watched. She stiffened when she saw my offering of a fresh fish and a rough bunch of wildflowers that I had picked on the way there and placed, very obviously, in the middle of the clearing.

Instantly, she dropped to all fours and sniffed the air around, her eyes darting this way and that like a wild animal sensing danger. I laughed to myself as I thought of those nature documentaries that I used to spend hours watching. Now, it felt like I was living a scene from one and it all seemed faintly surreal, even by the crazy standards of what my life had become.

I did nothing but watch, discreetly: caution was my reaffirmed mantra. After a sufficient time had passed, she decided that there was no immediate danger and took the fish back inside; she left the flowers where they lay, wilting in the mud.

I approached her home stealthily, half crawling, until I could smell cooking and even hear her singing softly to herself. I was so unbelievably sick of eating fish but somehow, the fish that *she* was making seemed different, more appealing. I was suddenly hungry, in a number of ways, and the aroma took me drifting off into a vivid daydream where we lived together in domestic bliss, and she was cooking the fish for me.

Unconsciously, I leaned forward in eager anticipation until a fallen twig snapped under the weight of my hand. She stopped singing instantly and I realised that I was in sudden, mortal danger. My daydream was a vision of a possible future, but my current reality was very different indeed.

I stood and made a break for it, heading directly for the cover of the trees at the edge of the small clearing. In my panic, I didn't think to zigzag, running straight ahead, and that was to prove a damaging mistake.

I had almost made the safety of the woods when a sudden stab of sharp pain bit into my left calf muscle. I stifled a shout as I fell, catching another mouthful of earth and then rolled immediately sideways, into the cover of the undergrowth.

Despite my injury, I knew I had to get up and away or I risked being finished off there where I lay, an easy target. I stood, wincing as I put weight on the leg, with a black feathered arrow shaft now sticking out of it, and half-limped, half-ran into the thicker trees ahead. I purposefully made a lot of noise so that she would know I was taking flight and was, therefore, no longer a danger. I hoped this would persuade her not to follow me.

I stopped to listen behind but heard no signs of pursuit, so I allowed myself to relax a little. Gritting my teeth at the pain shooting upwards from my injury, I somehow managed to slowly stagger home, flopping onto my bed as I assessed the damage to my leg.

Tending to the wound, I saw at once that it was not deep. The shaft itself was small and, judging from the lack of throbbing or burning, did not seem to be poisoned. That did not, however, stop it from hurting exquisitely.

I put a thick twig between my teeth and bit down hard as I pulled on the dart to remove it. I was expecting a struggle but, to my surprise, it was not barbed and came out smoothly, with only a minimal amount of blood. I boiled some water to sterilise it, then washed the wound carefully and applied an antiseptic ointment from a blue tube with faded lettering. I then bandaged it tightly.

As a test, I put a little weight on it, and it did not feel too bad. With luck, it should heal well and, despite the pain, would not be a serious setback. Clearly, it could have been much, much worse and I thanked whoever, or whatever, was watching out for me.

I hobbled over to my favourite spot on the riverbank and sat thinking for a while, trying to analyse my feelings as detachedly as possible. I felt a very strong attraction to my new 'friend', even though I suspected that this was nothing more than my chronic loneliness projecting itself upon her, probably as a means of creating some small sliver of hope for a non-solitary future. Despite the fact that she could well be my death and the sobering thought that she almost had been, on two separate occasions, I refused to give up.

I concluded, as I thought over the issue, that I had no real choice. I could be killed, but my chances of a long life were slim anyway, so I needed to convince her to trust me. At the same time, I could not allow my desperation to overrule caution, as it had done twice previously. That would be much easier said than done, however.

***

I took a few days to myself while I allowed my injury to heal. I eagerly settled back into my usual routine of fishing in the morning, eating a huge lunch and then drinking in the afternoon. I soon realised, however, that I was drinking much less than usual and there was an undeniable spring in my step, despite my sore leg, as I went about my daily life.

I was not completely sure, but I thought I recognised a faint glimmer of hope, a feeling that had been absent for many long, long years but was very welcome indeed. In fact, I was almost happy, as high on potential and possibility as I was distant from reality.

I sat by the riverside on the third night of my recuperation, with the ubiquitous glass of wine, and contemplated whether or not to reattempt contact the following day. As I thought about it, a knot of fear spasmed into existence, deep in my being, and began to slowly embed itself in my core. I realised that I had been living on anticipation but that was all it was, there was nothing concrete to it.

Hope was a wonderful state of mind but inherent in such a feeling was the very real possibility of not succeeding, which provided a sobering foil to counter the optimism. I realised that the prospect of failing terrified me more than anything else; if I did not succeed in this then I might never recover.

I had been living in the happy medium of future potential and the uncertainty of further action scared me to my very essence. As a counterpoint to this, I also knew that I had lived with fear as a constant companion for too long to allow it to win. I had nothing to lose and everything to gain but I needed to convince myself to take a chance and leave my comfort zone: literally and figuratively.

***

I sat and watched, well out of bow range, as she emerged from her home and noticed the gifts that I had again laid out for her, in the same way as previously. I was a little nervous but also hugely relieved that she hadn't upped sticks after our last encounter and moved away from the area, never to be seen again. I would certainly have left my refuge if I thought it had been compromised in any way.

Despite my elation that she had stayed, a little part of me could not help but wonder why: what had kept her there? I watched as she dropped to her knees and cocked an arrow, ready. She scoured the surroundings for danger, probably looking for me, but I was well-hidden this time and fully alert, so I had made sure that I could not be seen.

Eventually, she appeared to give up and shouted, "What do you want?" Her voice seemed shaky and unsure, as was mine when I replied.

"I just want to talk…to be friends."

As I formed the words, I realised that I could not remember the last time I had spoken to anyone. She looked puzzled for a second and lowered her bow, just a little.

"Why?" she said, eventually. I didn't really have an answer for that, so I thought a while and decided that honesty was the best way forward.

"Because it's better than being alone," I replied. She swung her bow suddenly round until it was pointing directly my way; she was good, getting me to talk to reveal my location. "That's not necessary," I protested, trying to sound jovial and friendly, although I barely remembered how to.

"I'll decide that, not you," she said, with a half-smile that was almost playful, but her words were quietly menacing, nonetheless.

"I'm unarmed," I offered by way of explanation, though that wasn't strictly true; my long knife was tucked into my waistband, as per usual. Naturally, I did not *want* to hurt her and would not willingly do so. What was more, I was sure that if she wanted to hurt me then I would already be dead. I just had to convince her that she did not need to be afraid.

She did not reply, so I tried again.

"I brought a bottle of wine."

"What?" Genuine surprise and confusion.

"Um…I thought maybe we could drink it together?"

She thought for a second.

"So you can get me drunk and have your way with me?" she snorted.

"No! No way!" I was indignant and more than a little offended. "I just thought it would be nice to share a drink and get to know each other," I offered, more gently. I saw that she was snickering to herself now, not wholly unkindly but a little incredulously, and I suddenly felt very foolish.

"Are you asking me *OUT*?" She sounded amazed.

I shrugged, then, remembering that she could not see me, mumbled, "Yeah, I suppose so."

She stifled a full-blown laugh and said, "Why should I say yes? You must think I'm desperate! I've never even seen your face properly."

Things were not really going well; it certainly had not played out like this in my mind. I'd thought she would be as lonely and miserable as I myself was and would therefore be bowled over by my humanity and kindness.

"If I stand up, will you promise not to shoot me?" I shouted, hopefully.

"Trust me," she grinned. I was in no way reassured but I had little choice, so I took a chance and got slowly to my feet with both hands empty and clearly visible, smiling like a curious child.

"Turn around," she commanded. I did a slow twirl for her, feeling faintly ridiculous and grinning shyly. "Cute smile," she said, "but too skinny and you *REALLY* need a shave. Nice accent, though." I just shrugged my shoulders and chuckled helplessly. I couldn't believe that I was being objectified so casually. Obviously, some vestigial traces of our former society remained within the both of us.

I attempted a laugh and then countered with, "Well, maybe *YOU* could brush your hair every once in a while and the occasional shower would not go amiss either but hey, nobody's perfect."

She laughed: a genuine, warm giggle and the sound was music to my ears. "You're right; things have changed a little in this game," she grinned.

"So…how about sharing that bottle of wine then? It's a good one," I suggested.

She looked up at the sky and said, "Now? Isn't it a little early?"

"Not now, of course! Later on, this evening." I backtracked quickly while still trying to sound as natural as possible. She didn't need to know that anytime was wine time in my world.

"Okay," she said after a moment's deliberation, "but we do it on my terms. Any funny business and you get an arrow in the neck." Her tone was deadly serious.

"I'll bear that in mind," I said, unaffected, and flashed the cheeky, lopsided smile that I remembered used to work fairly well, in another life.

"Come round about an hour before dark," she ordered, "and bring a glass, I've only got one."

"Right, see you later," I said nonchalantly and turned to head off home.

"Wait," she shouted, "one more thing."

"Yes?"

"Have a shave, would you?"

"Ha!" I snorted and sauntered off into the trees, leaving the wine behind and still not a hundred percent certain that she wouldn't shoot me in the back.

***

My teeth chattered as I reluctantly slipped into the icy depths of the river outside my home. We were in the height of summer, probably late June judging by the length of the days, but the water was still breathtakingly cold. I prided myself, among other things, on the fact that I still bathed. In my eyes, this elevated me way above most of the people left on Earth, or so it seemed. That did not mean, however, that I did it often.

To be washed and smell pleasant is a highly civilised attribute and I clung on to that notion stoically. In truth, however, I had grown somewhat lax of late regarding my personal hygiene. There seemed little point in keeping myself clean, only to immediately get dirty again foraging for supplies or hunting for food. In short, I subscribed to lofty ideals but had considerable difficulty adhering to them. That day, however, I was newly motivated and attacked my state of deep-ingrained filth with all the vigour of a man possessed.

I watched the shampoo that I had just washed off my head pool and then flow downstream. Years ago, I would have felt guilty about that but not anymore. One advantage of the decimation of the human population was that the river was now free of pollutants and cleaner than it had been in centuries. Our race was dwindling but the Earth was thriving with our decline.

Shaving, however, was very challenging with no mirror and over a year's worth of growth to hack off. I briefly considered the worth of doing it but the fact that she had specifically requested for me to remove the beard was motivation enough to persevere.

I eventually managed to achieve a relatively smooth face, getting through three plastic disposable razors in the process. Luckily, they were not highly prized loot items so would be easy to replace. More than a few drops of red had trickled down my neck and swirled away downstream but, running my hand over my largely clean cheeks, I knew it was worth it.

I got dressed in some old-style clothes that I hadn't put on for years but were much nicer than the rags I usually wore: a pair of jeans that were once the right size but hung off my skinny frame like curtains and a small t-shirt that could now easily shelter two of me. Finally, I liberally applied some eau de toilette, from a bottle of what had once been a globally popular, and expensive, brand.

I didn't need a mirror to know that I looked foolish, like a picture from a history book, trussed up like a prize turkey. Then, as I looked down at my trousers and my battered old sports shoes, I just felt scared and incredibly unsure of myself.

***

I approached cautiously, moving slowly and producing lots of noise to make my arrival obvious. The evening was getting old, but we still had a good hour or so of midsummer sunlight left.

"Hello? It's me," I shouted, as I emerged from the trees.

"Stay where you are," she commanded from across the clearing and I stood there, completely still, until she emerged from behind me, bow trained firmly on my back, catching me completely unawares.

"Were you followed? Are you alone?" she barked.

"No, and yes," I stammered, taken aback.

"How do I know this is not a trick?"

"Haven't we already done this?" I tried, with a cheeky grin.

"Answer the question," she cut me off, without a hint of mirth in her voice.

"I give you my word…trust me," I ventured, not even convincing myself. She snorted and half-snarled, half-laughed.

"Good joke, now sit down." She motioned to a spot in the middle of the clearing.

"Here?"

"Yes, unless you want to go home?"

"Um, not really." I was quite confused by now. "I brought a glass," I said, almost pitifully.

"Great, now, would you please sit down?" she ordered, though a little more lightly. I sat down on the floor while she circled around in front of my position, keeping her bow fully drawn as she looked me over.

"Any funny business and I shoot you between the eyes, got it?" she threatened.

"Understood," I replied, and placed my glass on the floor in front of where I was sitting.

She studied me for a few seconds, then said, "You look...old-fashioned." She, on the other hand, had not gone to much effort to prepare for tonight, though I thought I detected a hint of make-up.

"Well, I had a shave, at least," I protested.

"Yes, you did."

She backtracked a few paces until she was about three metres away, then exclaimed, "Okay. Perfect. Right, you sit there, don't move and I'll sit here." Then, she walked back to her hut without taking her eyes, or weapon, off me.

She went in to retrieve the bottle of wine I had given her and a glass from inside, then walked back to her spot on the grass and poured herself a measure, all, impressively, while still targeting me with her arrow. She moved fluidly, gracefully and assuredly: I was utterly captivated.

"Now, your turn," she said, screwing the cap back on the bottle and tossing it to me. I caught it awkwardly, wondering briefly if I should wipe it down before pouring but instead, I just opened it and poured myself a glass.

"You lied about it being a nice bottle. Nice bottles never used to have screw-tops," she admonished when I had finished.

"Well, it wasn't a lie, the bottle *IS* nice, engraved glass with a pretty label."

She, very kindly, laughed at my attempt at humour.

"I haven't heard a joke for years."

"That's why you're laughing at mine," I cracked and again she chuckled.

"So funny!" she groaned and rolled her eyes exaggeratedly.

"Easy crowd," I quipped, using an old favourite of mine. She laughed again.

"How about taking the weapon off me?" I enquired, suddenly.

"Hmm…convince me I should," she answered, measuredly. I didn't know how to reply to that, so I just smiled at her as I took a long swig of the wine, being pleasantly surprised by its quality.

"Well, talk," she commanded.

"Huh?" I snapped back to reality.

"You wanted to drink and talk, you've started drinking, now start talking."

I racked my brain then asked, "Do you come here often?" She paused a second then belly laughed at that and even lowered the bow a little.

"You cheesy bastard." She giggled and stuck her tongue out at me.

"It's a classic," I replied, grinning widely. I'd fancied myself a bit of a charmer in the old days, but this was ridiculously easy. Thankfully, it seemed increasingly likely that I was going to be able to avoid her providing my face with extra ventilation, courtesy of one of her arrows.

When she had stopped laughing, she took a long first swig of her wine, perhaps now satisfied that it wasn't poison, then looked me straight in the eyes and asked my name.

I was taken aback and I couldn't recall, at first, what it was; it had been many long years since my name had even been a consideration. Then, I relaxed as it all came flooding back in a wave of connections to the long-dead past. I smiled, eventually, and told her.

***

We talked for hours, until it became almost too dark to see each other and I realised that it was time to go. I reluctantly took my leave and began to walk home, a little unsteadily. She, on the other hand, had shown no sign of being affected by the alcohol at all, despite having drunk half a bottle and I was genuinely impressed. She definitely seemed to be a woman after my own heart.

I took a long, meandering route back. I was half-drunk on the wine and high on the company I had enjoyed and I did not want the feeling to end. Upon reaching home, I was too wired to sleep, so I delved into a tub of my vile homebrew, which I had made from some apple juice, yeast and sugar I had scavenged, and poured myself a glass to round off the evening.

It was disgusting, especially compared to the wine I had been drinking a scant half an hour ago, with sediment and unfermented yeast floating in hideous lumps and hanging in obscene suspension, but the buzz of the evening and the warm glow she had created in my spirit carried me through two full glasses of the hell water, sludge and all.

Eventually, when I could no longer keep my eyes open, nor focus on my hand in front of my face, I crawled into my hovel and collapsed on the bedding. I dropped immediately into an inebriated sleep, face down and fully clothed: shoes included.

I awoke the next day with a savagely pounding head, a mouth that felt like I'd been chewing sand all night and breath to curdle milk. I lay there in a kind of limbo for about an hour, thinking, dreaming of glasses full of cool, refreshing water but too lazy and nauseous to fetch any.

Finally, I dragged myself to my feet, stooped to exit my hovel and then staggered unevenly outside into the warmth and sunshine. I was immediately sick in the hedge that encircled my home, sinking to my knees as I heaved. In between retches and gulps of air, I cursed myself for having overdone it and spoiling a wonderful evening; I just did not know when, or how, to stop. In that moment, I remembered that a great ambience and a festive atmosphere only last until the morning after kicks in. In those days, I was well-familiar with hangovers but a little rusty when it came to feeling festive.

I pulled myself feebly to my feet and lurched on jelly knees, which threatened imminent collapse, through the foliage to the water's edge. I then poured a litre of clear, cool river water through my homemade strainer and into a large plastic bottle.

I didn't have the energy to boil it, as I usually would, and the first gulp I took reappeared almost instantly, splashing the earth between my shoes as I hurriedly jumped backwards. I took a few deep breaths, leaning on a tree trunk, then tried again and this time the water stayed down; I could almost feel it shooting through my bloodstream, like a silver bullet, and beginning the healing process. There was a long way to go before a full recovery, however, and I realised that the rest of the day would be a complete write-off as I crawled gladly back into bed.

***

I woke again, what seemed like hours later, and sat up very slowly, waiting for the expected throb of agony to spasm through my head but, to my surprise, it did not come and I allowed myself a tiny smile of relief. My mouth still felt parched, but another long drink of water would surely sort that out.

As I emerged from the sunken doorway on my knees, I saw that though the sun was much lower in the sky, it was still warm and light. Staggering towards the river to quench my thirst, I watched my shadow flit over the rough ground and thought about her. Now that the fog and pain clouding my head had cleared, she came crashing back to fill my consciousness once more.

As I swallowed a full bottle of crystal-clear river water and gnawed on a hunk of smoked fish, which I was not a hundred percent sure would stay in my stomach, I resolved to go and see her again that evening. The rules of this game had changed beyond all recognition, as had our entire world, and I did not want to risk anything by doing nothing.

After a quick wash in the shallows, my second in as many days, I got dressed in something a bit more modern: stained rags and handmade shoes, and set off for her place.

I proceeded a little more cautiously through the sunlit woods than I had on previous trips to her home. The ardent fervour and blinkered focus of the last few days had subsided somewhat and been replaced by a return to brutal reality. They were perilous times and hope and positivity alone would not protect me.

I did not want to lose my head and expose myself to unnecessary danger. That would achieve nothing, especially now I was starting to feel that I might have something to lose. Almost in mockery of my caution, however, everything seemed unbelievably normal as I strode purposefully and stealthily through the evening forest, an ethereal being on an age-old mission.

As I approached her home, I paused, feeling a sudden unease. Long years in the woods, hunting and surviving, had taught me to read its sights, sounds and smells intuitively and I definitely knew something was wrong.

I stopped dead, neither making a sound nor moving and I realised that the animals around me, too, were completely silent. The insects hummed, sang and buzzed, oblivious as usual, but no birdsong. That usually meant that there was danger in the immediate area and they had either flown away or were in hiding. I could see nothing, however, from my position on the forest floor, so I very stealthily moved across to the nearest climbable tree and shimmied up it expertly, without a sound.

I scanned the area around her home and immediately saw something strange, directly in front of her 'door'. Not for the first time, I thanked my surgically enhanced eyes as they automatically adjusted to enable me to see, in high detail, what it was, despite being so far away.

In the middle of the clearing, laid out on a tattered piece of cloth, was the carcass of an animal, though I could not tell which species. A cold chill coursed through my body when I recognised it as being exactly the same method I had used to gain her trust, except that this time it was not me. Someone was copying my crude strategy and that, surely, could not be a coincidence.

There was no sign of her, however, and I fervently hoped that she was merely staying indoors, away from danger. The trouble was, I could not see any sign of a threat, nor attackers, so I watched the scene for a few minutes, hoping any assailants would give themselves away by moving.

Out of the corner of my eye, I saw a sudden flicker of motion to the right and was able to pinpoint a man, gesturing silently across the clearing from among the trees. Then, the signal was answered with another flash of noiseless movement from the forest behind her home.

I thought their positions were strange, until it hit me with an awful realisation: they were obviously using the meat as bait to lure her out. Then, the second man would emerge from behind the dwelling to catch her by surprise, with the first man acting as a diversion out front for her deadly bow.

They obviously did not want to kill her. A full and devastating assault would be most effective if that were the case, and she would, most likely, already be dead by now. Clearly, they wanted her alive and it did not take a genius to guess as to what purpose; I highly doubted that they were seeking companionship and romance, as I was.

I could see that both men were armed, their blades gleaming intermittently in the evening sun, but neither seemed to have a gun or bow, which was something at least. I fought to keep my cool against a rising tide of boiling blood, which raced through my veins and filled me with a murderous rage. I needed to keep calm. I had to act coolly and quickly.

Silently, I slid down the tree and crept round to the first man's position. He was not expecting an attack from behind and was solely focusing his attention on the clearing and his partner. He had no chance.

I slunk up behind him, perfectly stealthily, drawing my trusty knife from my waistband as I approached within striking range. I stepped forward and, with a practised ease, wrapped one hand around his mouth, so he could not shout, and slit his throat cleanly with the blade in the other.

Immediately, I released my grip and pushed his body away, to avoid the blood that pumped out in instant, terrible jets from the new hole in his neck. He fell onto his back, making a gurgling noise, and his dying eyes stared at me, accusingly, as he choked and writhed his life away on the earth at my feet. I held his gaze for a brief second but could not maintain it and averted my eyes out of respect, or maybe shame; I knew not which.

Once the man's retinas had completely glazed over in the finality of death, I moved quickly around to tackle the other aggressor, lying in wait behind her house, thinking that he, too, would have no chance against an unexpected attack. As I got closer, however, I realised with trepidation that there was open ground all around his position and I would not be able to get close enough for a surprise kill. I would have to throw my knife instead.

Although I had, by now, had much more practice hunting small animals in the woods and was far more adept at throwing a blade than I had previously been, all I could think of was the first knife I'd ever thrown, an age ago back in the city, and I resolved not to miss this time.

Each occasion, as it was then, the situation and the players were different, but it was all part of a larger routine, which had played itself out countless times since our descent into savagery. I hefted the weapon in my palm, feeling its perfect balance and gripped the point, sizing up the shot. Then, I threw it in a single, swift motion at my target.

The knife sank inexorably into his throat, blossoming like a sudden, devastating flower and catching him completely unawares. He let out a strangled attempt at a cry and sank to his knees, clutching at his neck as his life ebbed away. He pulled the blade out feebly and let it fall through crimson-stained fingers as his eyes, heavy with surprise and fear, fixed on the blood now arcing away from his neck in rapid, red spurts.

Mercifully, he did not take long to die but I still stood and watched his body for a long while, wracked with inner turmoil. I'd read that it got easier to kill people, the more you did it, but my experience had proved that to be a lie.

It was relatively easy to end a life in a sudden, knife-edge moment but it never got any easier to process when one looked back at their actions later on. Thinking beyond the savages that they had evidently become, these men were still human: still people, with hopes, fears, dreams, ambitions and a unique character, however repugnant. What right had I, or anyone else, to cut another's life short?

I knew the answer of course, the question was rhetorical, but I had to ask myself anyway. Perhaps in the asking alone I could claim a little remnant of humanity.

In truth, I could have walked away and they would then still be alive, but *she* might no longer be. I had made a choice, valuing one life over two others and I had chosen to kill in order to conserve that life.

I looked down at my hands, flecked with congealing blood, and wondered whether any of the sins that I had committed were truly worth it, or was I merely lying to myself, justifying homicide with a hideous charade of noble ideals?

I had hidden myself away from human contact to avoid that very dilemma and there I was murdering again, killing in cold blood for a chance at companionship, killing for personal gain. I spat at the ground, cursing the world for forcing my hand and cursing myself doubly for allowing myself to become such a hollow paradox of a person.

With an extreme effort, I pulled myself away from the inviting precipice of insanity, wiping my hands on the ground as I approached her home.

"It's okay, it's safe now," I ventured in the direction of her house.

"Who's that?" she replied instantly. She was obviously watching and listening intently.

"It's me, from last night, with the wine," I shouted.

"What do you want? Why are you here?"

"I came to see you."

"Why? You betrayed me to your *friends*. It was obviously all part of your plan. You must think I'm stupid."

"No, I swear, I don't know them. They must have been watching us all the time and then copied me," I protested.

"Bullshit," she spat.

"I can prove it. I killed them and now you're safe."

"Why should I believe you? How many were there?"

"Only two."

"Men?"

"Of course."

"What did they want?"

"I don't think I need to spell it out, but they were armed and *they* didn't seem to be carrying a bottle of wine."

"Right, prove it, then," she challenged, emerging from her home but crouched in the entrance, with her bow strung and aimed directly at me.

She was taking a chance by revealing herself, which may have meant that she believed me, if only a little. I went back round behind her house, to the closest body, and dragged the dead man by his feet into her line of sight, dropping him in front of her with a theatrical flourish. I then fetched the first corpse in the same manner and dumped him next to his erstwhile comrade, making a quick check, out of age-old habit, for any signs of infection but seeing none. I was panting from the exertion but grinned at her, despite the macabre situation.

"All yours!" I smiled, ecstatic just to be in her presence again. She looked at the bodies, then me, then at the bodies again.

"So…you're a killer, too?" she said after a long silence. It was half question, half allegation.

"Yes…I suppose I am," I whispered, looking down at my feet as my smile evaporated: I'd finally said it aloud.

"And you did that for me?" Her voice had softened.

"Yes, I thought you were in danger," I mumbled, meekly.

"You could have joined them and shared the spoils."

"No, that's not the kind of person I am," I proffered quietly, painfully aware of the hypocrisy in my words.

She laughed softly, thought a while then lowered her bow, looked at the bodies and said, "You know, I preferred it when you brought me wine."

I slowly realised she was making a joke and a small smile spread and then congealed across my face. She emerged fully from her hut, still holding her bow, but no longer trained on me. She looked over my handiwork a little more closely and concluded, "Nicely done, though a little messy, that's why I use a bow."

I inadvertently winced and rubbed my calf when she mentioned that and she noticed.

"Oh, yeah, sorry about that," she sighed, nonchalantly.

"That's okay, it was more of an inconvenience than anything else," I conceded.

"Luckily for you, I wanted to trust you, so the arrow wasn't poisoned nor even full size."

"Yeah, *thanks*," I said, slightly petulantly, then laughed a little.

"Anyway, I know it's a little soon, but how about moving in together?" she asked suddenly.

"Here?" I replied, a little taken aback.

"No, at your place. You live by the river, very nice, and it's plenty big enough for us both."

"How do you know that?" I was incredulous now.

"I followed you home when you were drunk." She winked at me.

"Wow, well, in that case, of course you can." I felt a sudden wave of genuine admiration and affection for this lady.

When she had collected her few, meagre possessions and I had reclaimed my knife, we hauled the two bodies on top of her hut and set fire to the mound. There was no sentimentality to her as we watched the flames engulf her former home and would-be captors.

Then, we walked together through the woods to my place, with her leading the way and me following, beaming widely at every tree we passed.

***

I emerged tentatively out into the pristine calm of the early morning, leaving behind the warmth of our home. The mist was milling gently on the river's surface and the frost dusted the ground in a savagely beautiful sheen of winter white.

The cold ground made my bare feet ache to the bones, with a stinging chill, and the freezing air bit at my exposed arms and legs but I was happy; my spirit was warm. I could see and smell the first signs of spring in the air and with it came a feeling of delirious hope.

I ducked inside and crawled gently back into the warmth of our bed. She stirred and half opened her eyes, murmuring something. She took my hand and placed it on her stomach to feel the life growing, kicking inside. I cracked a wide, wide smile as I locked my arms around her and allowed the comforting tendrils of sleep to drag me down, once more, into blissful rest.

Downriver

That one was definitely a scream. I could not roll over in my sleeping bag and ignore it any longer. It was probably a female voice, maybe even a child's, though it was very hard to be sure. I was still a little disorientated from the deep, dreamless slumber I'd been in and could not tell exactly where it was coming from but, even so, I still had a fair idea of its origins.

From where I was, I could see nothing through the thick trees, despite the sunlight shining brilliantly through the canopy to the floor beneath me. I shook the residual sleep out of my body and peeled myself out of the light camping bag that I'd scavenged earlier that summer, in preparation for this trip.

Folding my bedding quickly and stuffing it into my trusty pack that was hanging from a lower branch, I scrambled further up the tree, which had been providing me with a place to rest, to see if I could spot anything over the dense treetops but no luck. All that was visible was a vast expanse of green, framed by the sparkling, clear waters of the river to my left and the exquisitely blue sky overhead. There was no time to admire the view, beautiful as it was, for the scream came again, clearer and louder in my fully alert state, from a little deeper into the nameless wood that I had, fatefully, chosen as my resting place for the day.

Straining my augmented eyesight to its absolute limit, I could just make out a tiny drift of smoke rising, almost invisibly, through the thick leaves and intertwined branches. It was coming from a small clearing in roughly the same direction as the origin of the distress call. I knew that could not be a coincidence; it had to be the source of the scream.

Evidently, I had no idea what I was going to find, nor indeed what I was going to do once I got there, just a vague notion of duty to a fellow human seemingly in trouble. Many lonely, wine-soaked nights had been spent in dreaming of being a saviour, a chance to prove my enduring nobility by slaying the savage regressive but suddenly, the reality was upon me, and it did not feel like an opportunity for glory, it just felt frightening. Neither did I feel in any way like a hero. I felt nothing but tired and underprepared.

Still, fate chose its moments, not the other way round, so I dropped out of the tree, as silently as an olden-day ninja, and sped back to where my canoe was pulled ashore and camouflaged expertly, thereby hiding all clues as to my presence.

Reaching under the seat, I pulled out my fishing spear: a steel blade that I had strapped and mounted onto a shoulder-high, sturdy stick, and hefted it with a familiar ease. It was as good a weapon as I would ever need, equally as effective against human scumbags that infested the area as against river fish, who had reclaimed a once-polluted part of their watery world.

The scream came again, louder this time, as I ran towards its general direction. The tone had changed, somewhat, now sounding somewhat muffled and that worried me even more than before. I increased my pace, trying to balance the need for speed with the necessity of avoiding detection. I was well aware that I could be walking into a trap.

I slowed my pace as I tasted a sudden mouthful of acrid smoke, which told me I was nearing the source of the cries. Ahead, I could see light through the trees, which had to be the small clearing I had spotted earlier, and as I approached it, I could smell the fumes from the fire much more strongly.

I ducked quickly behind a huge tree as I heard voices, then I risked a look around the trunk to assess both the situation and my odds. What I saw made my blood run cold and an instant, apoplectic rage exploded into being in every ounce of my consciousness. I hoisted my harpoon and charged out: a soundlessly screaming, avenging arrow.

***

I had been travelling by night and hiding myself high in the trees during the day, to catch what sleep I could, but it was difficult to suddenly become nocturnal when one was used to sleeping after sundown. Despite the physical shock, doing this was necessary. I needed to be very discreet as I travelled. A craft travelling downriver was highly visible in daylight but almost impossible to see in the dark and I had, as a necessity for hunting, already mastered the art of paddling silently. It had helped me catch fish and now it was helping to keep me safe.

My canoe, which was an infinite improvement on the last boat I'd owned, was camouflaged with a dark brown coloured coating, so that when I pulled it ashore in the first rays of morning light and hid it among the foliage lining the riverbank, it was very hard to detect. If one were actively looking, then of course it would be found but I always made my camp far enough away from its location to be able to hear any trouble, and make my escape, before I myself was discovered.

Each morning, I made my bed high above the ground, among the boughs of the numerous lush trees that bordered the water. This meant constant back pain and broken nights of sleep. I'd even fallen once, two nights ago, and considered myself lucky to have only a sprained wrist to show for my misfortune.

Despite the many disadvantages of sleeping in the trees, it meant I was concealed and, therefore, safe. I would gladly trade a million great nights of rest on the ground for the feeling of security that hiding among the branches afforded, so I suffered and grabbed what repose I could, perched up high. Caution was my mantra, as always, but the lengths I took to avoid my fellow humans only served to highlight the essential paradox at the very heart of this bizarre downriver odyssey.

I had lived and survived alone for a good many years since my escape from the virus-ravaged city but I had never realised, foolishly, that the solitude was slowly poisoning me. Long months, even years, went by where I couldn't remember the last time that I'd had contact with any other human and most of the encounters I did have ended rapidly in either flight or violence.

Then, I'd met a woman last summer and had known the comfort of companionship and trust: real, human emotions, for the best part of a year but I'd been forced to watch her die as I stood by, ignorant and impotent, lacking the knowledge to even ease her suffering but feeling every shudder of her pain-wracked body in the depths of my soul. All I could do was hold her hand and weep softly as she left me alone in guilt-wracked anguish.

To think that I, through our love, was responsible for her death only made a bitter pill taste even worse. Thus, in the midst of a blossoming new spring, surrounded by the promise of new life and warmer weather, I found myself alone in grief, devoid of all hope and wishing only for my own demise. I made two makeshift wooden grave markers, the best I could manage, to decorate the freshly dug earth and hit the bottle again, harder than ever, seeking only oblivion.

Gradually, spring burgeoned into summer and the grief began to clear a little. I decided that *surviving* would be the ultimate revenge on fate, so determined in its cruelty. Essentially, I had not been destroyed by what had happened, but neither was I sure if I was stronger. My desperation was steadily being replaced by the cold realisation that I needed somewhere to *belong*.

I was beginning to understand that I, too, was a social creature, despite my professed misanthropy. Consequently, I had decided to set off downriver in search of something. I did not know what I would find but anything other than mind-numbing, desolate isolation would be an improvement.

We'd talked, many times, about heading north to a place she'd heard of, once our baby was born. That had been the plan until our future was so cruelly curtailed. Now, even as desperate as I was, I could not face that journey alone. Equally, I did not consider going upriver, towards the city, for even a second. I had barely escaped there with my life, years ago, and God only knew what horrors were to be found in and around its environs.

I had lived, for a while after fleeing my city home, by the sea in an old shipwreck, run aground on a reef. The coast attracted people of all persuasions and I knew that I would find some human contact there. I hopefully clung to the vague notion that I would discover something more than the regressed remnants of humanity I had previously encountered, perhaps a small village or some other vestige of civilisation to offer myself to and, therefore, provide my life with some kind of meaning, some kind of purpose.

Many a time, before the virus came, I had wished for solitude and dreamed idly of the blissful isolation that the end of the world would bring. I had grown sick of living among my fellow people, jostling for position, in both a literal and social sense. I had cursed humanity and yearned, petulantly, for the very desolation that was eating away relentlessly at what was left of my civilised soul.

In an unexpected twist of fate, my idle wish had become both my reality and my living nightmare. I found it cruelly ironic that I was actually planning on risking my life to search out the very human connections I had once bemoaned. Nevertheless, I had packed a few meagre possessions in my camouflaged canoe, scavenged a sleeping bag from an old camping store and headed off downriver.

***

I burst into the clearing and buried my harpoon deep into the back of a large man, who was lying, naked, on top of a barely visible, struggling victim. The well-sharpened blade slid in easily and drove deep, aiming for the heart, until it juddered to a halt as it struck bone. I quickly wrenched it out before it could snap, as the man started to scream and writhe beneath me.

He rolled over, away from my attack and off the figure underneath, which was clearly a young girl. The red mist descended further when I saw his victim, and obvious excitement, and I struck again, catching him a glancing blow on the neck as he desperately tried to scrabble away. Blood immediately started to gush out and his hands flew to the wound in a vain attempt to hold in his life. I knew then that his resistance was finished, so I pivoted to face my other adversary, who was standing a little away from the action.

This man was much smaller and scrawnier than his soon-to-be-deceased friend and, as he looked first at me, then at his companion, he rapidly decided to about turn and flee, as quickly as he possibly could. He did not look back, even once, as he made his desperate escape into the sanctuary of the dense trees.

I turned my gaze back to the first man, who was contorted on the floor, still futilely trying to staunch the blood, which was flowing from the jagged wounds in his back and neck. He turned his face towards me and his eyes were filled with pain and impotent malevolence, glaring as he coughed bloody globules of phlegm onto his filthy, matted chest hair. As I watched his struggles, my rage subsided and the familiar remorse quickly set in.

He was clearly beyond any help that I could give him, so I gently leant down and offered him a little water, from an earthen jug near the fire. He took a sip as best he could, then spat it back in my face as his eyes glazed over in the finality of death. *Fair enough*, I thought, as I carefully wiped the red-stained water from my skin with a filthy sleeve, making sure not to get any of the foul mixture in my eyes or mouth, just in case.

Turning my attention to the girl, I saw that she had retreated and was cowering against a tree, watching me from between her fingers with true fear in her face. Her gaze never left me.

I made a small move towards her and she edged away in terror. I stole a quick glance down at myself and saw what she was seeing: I was covered in blood and clutching a dripping weapon in my gore-stained fingers.

Gently, so as not to alarm her, I put the harpoon down and wiped my hands clean on the ground. Then, I raised them, with open palms.

"I won't hurt you," I said, as warmly as I could muster. She did not answer, just continued to stare at me, wide-eyed.

"I just saved your life," I tried again.

"I didn't need saving," she said eventually, meekly, "and you just killed my father."

***

After a short while watching me but making no attempt to run away, she took some of the food that I had cooked on the remnants of the fire. I did not really want to linger in that place but neither could I, ethically, leave the girl there alone, so I attempted to gain her trust. I kept the harpoon ready, however, just in case the other man returned with reinforcements.

The girl was still studying my every move intently, though she had taken her hands from her eyes and seemed a lot more relaxed than before. Then, she glanced down at the food in her lap for a moment and I took the opportunity to give her a long look-over, without causing any further alarm.

She looked young, maybe twelve or thirteen, but it was very hard to tell. Nobody I saw was exactly well-nourished and it was very possible that she was older but just small for her age. Her hair was long and unkempt and hung in greasy streaks down each side of her grubby face. She had no obvious signs of infection: it was rare indeed by then, but caution had long been my byword and I was always alert. She sensed me looking and lifted her head, staring back at me.

Her eyes were piercing, obsidian pits that fixed me with a stare that seemed old, way before its time, and belied her youthful appearance. They were hard, calculating: the eyes of a survivor. God only knew what horrors she'd seen already in her short life but there was, yet, a spark of fierce defiance and pride there that burrowed directly into the soul. Though her stance was submissive and unassuming, those eyes seemed to tell the full story of the price she had paid, thus far, for her survival.

I could not hold her gaze without seeing the depths of my own twisted soul reflected back at me, so I glanced down. She wore a shapeless, tattered robe, but if her arms and face were anything to judge by, then the rest of her was equally as stick thin. She looked so frail and helpless sitting there that it was hard to imagine any man, even these days, having anything other than paternal feelings for her. Judging by her previous ordeal, however, this was obviously not the case.

"Are you deciding whether or not to kill me?" she asked, finally.

"No, of course not, I told you before, I won't hurt you."

"But you killed my father," she pointed out and nodded in the direction of the deep thicket, where I had dragged the body, away from where we were eating, and then she looked at the blood, which stained the grass in large spatters.

"And you would have killed that other man, too, if he hadn't run away," she said, somewhat accusingly. I just shrugged my shoulders helplessly; I had no answer for that.

"Why don't you want to kill *me*?"

"I don't like killing people, I only do it when I have to," I replied, though I sounded especially weak and unconvincing, even to myself.

"Did you *need* to kill him?" She again nodded towards the bushes.

"Yes, he was hurting you," I said, as emphatically as I could muster.

"No, he wasn't, and I would have been okay. It happened before, lots of times."

"Why were you screaming, then?"

"For the other guy, he liked me to scream."

"Who was he?" I asked, a little incredulously.

"Some guy who lived nearby. He gave us food if he could watch, and it helped us out. He was a bit weird, kind of creepy but he was okay." She finished eating, then looked around nonchalantly.

"You talk kind of strangely," she said, abruptly.

"Well, I'm not from these parts, I'm from another country," I replied, caught off-guard by the sudden change in topic.

"What's a *coun-try*?" she asked, like a child to a parent.

"It's another place, over the sea." I could tell by her face that this was way beyond her comprehension, so I simplified.

"I'm from far away."

"Okay."

That seemed to satisfy her curiosity.

"How old are you?"

I tried to make conversation. I never imagined, in all my idle, wine-fuelled dreams by the river, that just talking to another person could be so strange and so difficult. She merely shrugged her shoulders and studied the ground at her feet.

"Your father never told you?" I was a little shocked, all children loved telling you how old they were and counting the months until their next birthday; the children I used to know anyway.

"He told me he found me when I was tiny and looked after me."

Probably after he raped and killed her mother, I thought.

"He wasn't your real father, then?"

"He said he was. I think he was. What do you mean?"

I was starting to realise, as I talked to her, just how much the world had changed since its 'end', and it was rapidly becoming clear exactly how out of touch I was with the way things operated. I was an anachronism, a man out of time and now out of place, thanks to this half-baked plan of mine. I was beginning to seriously question the validity of holding onto old ideals if they were, clearly, no longer relevant.

"It doesn't matter," I said, finally. "It's getting dark. We should probably get going."

"Where? Where are we going?" She looked confused.

"Home, to my house. You can live with me. I'll look after you."

"But I'd rather stay here," she replied, plaintively. Her tone was childlike, pleading and her body language deferential but her eyes were pure steel as they fixed me, unwaveringly.

"Well, I can't stay here with you, and I can't leave you here alone," I said, with a view to ending the discussion.

"Why not?"

"Because you won't be safe alone."

"But I want to stay here. I don't know anywhere else."

"I can't leave you here. You're coming with me. That's final."

"So, I belong to you, now. My father used to say that to me, too."

"No, this isn't the same! I'm different to him. You don't *belong* to me."

"No, it isn't different! You're taking me with you, somewhere I don't want to go. So, I'm your prisoner."

"It's not like that, honestly, I'm going to protect you."

"But I don't *want* to go with you, and you are forcing me to go with you. I have no choice, so I'm your prisoner," she said, forcefully now. I didn't really have an answer for that. She had a point and she definitely knew it.

Clearly, she wouldn't understand it from my perspective. The things I'd seen, I knew she wouldn't last long. I also knew that there was no use arguing with adolescents, so I just collected our meagre belongings, then motioned for her to follow me back to the river and my camp. She hung back for a second, looking sullenly defiant, then shrugged her shoulders and followed.

***

I took her back with me, to near where my canoe was and told her that we needed to rest. She acquiesced surprisingly quickly and I showed her how to climb up a tree and make a bed among its branches. I only had one sleeping bag, so I let her use it; it was warm enough anyway in the late afternoon sun.

We settled down for a few hours of sleep, before night fell and we would set off, back upriver to my home. I hadn't thought about what would happen when we got there but, for the time being, all I could think of was closing my eyes for a rest. For a few long minutes I could hear her turning and muttering to herself incessantly on the branch next to me. Sleep was impossible.

"Are you okay?" I asked finally, exasperated.

"I'm not tired, and you're weird, sleeping in the day, up a tree, like a monster or something." She sounded wide-awake.

"Like a vampire, you mean?" I chuckled, ruefully.

"A what?"

"Forget it. Just try and get some sleep, we're going to be travelling all night." There was silence for a brief second.

"I'm cold," she changed the subject.

"How can you be? It's really warm today."

"Dunno, just am. Hey…can I come and sleep with you?"

I was about to say no when she was suddenly lying next to me on my branch, her arms snaking around my body, her hands wandering. I hesitated for a split-second: it had been such a long time since I had last been touched, but I knew it was wrong.

"What are you *doing*?" I pleaded, trying to disentangle her from my most private areas. Her hands never stopped.

"You saved me, you said so. I want to thank you."

"You don't have to do *that*," I said firmly and managed to hold on to her wrists and restrain them from any further travelling.

"You know you like it and I need to *thank* you." She sounded a little confused and unsure now.

"You don't and I don't, honestly. You're too young. It's wrong." Her hands went suddenly limp. My voice was full of disgust at the situation. I was appalled at what she was doing. It was evidently the only way she knew of interacting with adults and clearly spoke of a childhood of non-stop abuse.

I was thinking all this but she just saw and heard the revulsion in my voice and thought it was directed at her. She shuffled backwards, away from me, and her face fell, hurt, a lost, confused little girl.

"I didn't mean it like that," I apologised but she just looked away and did not reply.

"I'm sorry. Please try and get some sleep," I said, gently and she crawled back to her branch, got into the sleeping bag and rolled over with her back to me. I sighed and lay for a while, thinking, before closing my eyes and drifting into sleep's welcoming oblivion.

***

I woke with a start. The evening was drawing in and the sun was sinking low in the sky, casting shadows all around the tree I was lying in. It was time to move on. I sat up and called to her, but there was no answer. I glanced across to the branch where she had been sleeping but there was nobody there. I did a double-take and looked around but she was still nowhere to be seen, neither was my bag that had been hanging in the lower branches of the tree. All of my supplies: my tools, my bedding and even my beloved harpoon were gone. She had left and taken all my stuff with her as I slept.

I cursed as I jumped out of the tree to check if my canoe was still there. Luckily, it was, and I dragged it out from its concealment and onto the riverbank. I now had nothing and with no supplies: no food, no water, no hunting tools, there was nothing else I could do but turn around and go upriver, as quickly as possible, back to where I could find rest, shelter, provisions and weapons.

I had to go home.

Extinction

The stone glistened in the sun as I turned it, over and over, idly in my hands, the light catching its polished faces and accentuating its still-sharp edges. The thing was still usable, in spite of the long, long years it had lain in the ground. I thought about the ancient hands that had fashioned, and then used, that prehistoric axe.

The owner of those hands might well be long-dead, and their world vanished, but the individual who made the tool in my palm was from a species on the ascent, a species with unlimited potential. They would not have known it but their race was already branching out into new environments and inventing new technologies on its way to taming the world.

The hands that were holding that piece of ancient ingenuity belonged to a member of a race very much in decline and that decline was, most likely, to prove terminal. Hard to believe, then, that both individuals belonged to the same species and that a mere forty thousand years or so was all that separated them.

We had achieved so much in an evolutionary blink of the eye: space colonisation, instant communications, the virtual eradication of true poverty, triumph over disease (present situation notwithstanding) and sizeable extensions to our natural lifespan. The list was so long and illustrious that it was nothing but a source of immense pride for all who considered it. We had finally transcended our animal origins and shaken ourselves free of selfish, instinctive destructiveness. We had successfully avoided our species' inevitable warrior doom. Or so we had led ourselves to believe.

The sickness hit so quickly that nobody even had time to give it a name, neither scientific nor common. It was just known and referred to as 'the virus'. Despite the widespread death, panic and horror that it caused, it wasn't the disease itself that rang the death knell for our society.

With more than eight billion people choking the surface of the Earth, it would have taken something on an immensely destructive scale to drive our species to extinction. The law of averages dictated that a certain percentage of humanity would be immune to any infection, and therefore survive, and even if that was only a fraction of one percent, then they would still have numbered in their millions.

Indeed, the virus's spread and aggressiveness dictated that anyone who remained alive would probably be either immune themselves or the progeny of the immune. In terms of a threat to our species' future, the pathogen had, years since, ceased to be a going concern, apart from the odd, isolated case, it seemed.

What happened in reality, though, is that the virus brought us to the brink of a panic, where all the ugliest aspects of human nature pushed and clawed their way, screaming, to the fore of our being and dictated our interactions with each other from then on.

We thought we had sublimed but we were complacent, and our civilisation was quickly revealed as nothing but a thin veneer, stretched too tightly across the raging animal within. With the pandemic providing a strong enough push, the facade cracked and the beast escaped. Pacifists became murderers, the virtuous became thieves and the free spirited became mindless sheep, following the nearest demagogue. In reality, the virus hanged us, but we drew and quartered ourselves.

Without the benefit of this bitter hindsight, nobody, not even the greatest thinkers of the time, could ever have dreamed how truly fragile our society was. If one thought themselves invincible, then one made no contingency plan for failure and that proved our undoing in the short term and, more than likely, would prove to be our doom in the not-too-distant future.

Tellingly, I had not seen many living children on my travels, but I had seen many, many of their corpses, more than I could realistically ever hope to keep a tally of. I saw harbingers of our death wherever I travelled.

Every single human demise was a miniature tragedy, which our species could not afford. We were endangering our very existence with murderous self-centredness and short-sighted greed. We stood on the verge of an early exit, and at our own hands. How ironic that we, who were the cause of countless other extinctions in the past, were now pushing ourselves to its very brink.

Even were we to survive as a species, I was afraid that society, civilisation and all their inherent achievements had already followed the infamous dodo into the oblivion of history: long dead and never to return. I saw precious little evidence of cultured behaviour, or basic decency, in my rare human encounters.

Distrust, a fear of others, was the enemy of any civilised person, that much I was sure of. I was also sure, however, that my fellows would think the same about me as I about them: that I was a savage, barbaric killer. Paradoxically, I myself feared that I might be the last shred of human decency alive, a dying breed, for sure. If I met my end alone, there, then I genuinely believed that the last true bearer of the metaphorical torchlight of humanity, as we knew it, would be extinguished.

I had to do something.

Convenience

'The road is long, but our coffee is strong'.

I looked quizzically down at the tattered piece of card, clutched tightly in my filthy fingers, bearing those faded, hand-written letters. The grubby little memento, from a warmth I once knew, seemed to have very little to do with the real place that I could see below me, albeit only vaguely, in the blackness of the very early morning.

It existed. I knew for certain, for I had seen it with my own eyes and, at last, I believed. I had thought it nothing but a dream, the promise of a flicker of light in our ever-encroaching darkness for a pair of hapless souls to hold on to, an impossible ideal. This place had been a reason to live for, something to keep the hope alive but I must admit that, in my bitter cynicism, I had doubted it was real. I doubted no more.

There I stood, a solitary figure gazing out over the promised land, and I could see it, in the near distance, from my vantage point high among the overlooking trees. A faint, yet obvious, twinkle of artificial light, where there should not be any, in an otherwise stygian panorama.

At that ungodly hour of the night, the compound was undoubtedly closed but I knew it would surely open again in the morning. I decided to try and snatch a few hours of sleep and then wind my way down, in the first rays of the sun, for a steaming hot cup of our civilised past.

***

At very first light, I broke my pathetic little camp: a mouldy sleeping bag and a mildewed backpack, balanced precariously between the branches of a large tree that had already lost most of its leaves to the oncoming winter.

Standing absolutely still for a long instant, I listened and sensed the crisp morning air around me for any signs of movement, or atmosphere of unease among the wildlife. Finally, satisfied that I was alone and therefore safe, I crept down through the trees to retrieve my bicycle from its hiding place, among the deep foliage that thronged the banks of the highway. The road had once belonged to a network that was the nation's arteries, carrying commerce and supplies its length and breadth. Now, such thoroughfares were merely magnets for thieves and murderers.

In light of this, I always made camp half a kilometre, at least, away from my trusty vehicle to avoid, or at least lessen, the chance of detection. The area seemed safer and less populated than further south but I was not about to take any chances, nor make any more stupid mistakes, at this late stage of my northbound odyssey.

I mounted gingerly, still sore from the long journey, easing my aching posterior into the saddle and, not for the first time, regretting my reliance on the bicycle, as opposed to something with an engine and four wheels.

The motorways were still in a fairly good state of repair, even after so many years of neglect, which was testament to the sophistication of their design and the quality of their construction. It was still very slow-going riding in the dark, however, and sleeping high up in the trees was rougher than my bed, in the home I'd left behind, which was luxurious by comparison.

The morning was in its infancy, silent and stark, and I was fairly sure that any human scumbags in the area would not be up and about for a good few hours at least. Rape, murder and theft really took it out of them and they needed their rest.

I clicked my bicycle into gear and set off down the road, trying to shake the deep ache from my legs. The tarmac ahead was smooth and uncracked, mercifully, and I once again gave silent thanks that at least highways had survived, a remnant of the society that once was, and a very useful remnant at that. The fact that traffic was now almost non-existent certainly helped with their preservation, too.

Despite my complaints, cycling was by far the safest, and hence the best, method of travel, in my opinion. Bicycles used no fuel and were easy to maintain, which made them preferable to a car any day, and there was no need to scavenge or raid for propellant. They were also quiet and travelling by bike was much quicker than walking. In addition, on a bright, clear, sunny morning, such as this one was rapidly becoming, despite the cold, it was even highly enjoyable. The gentle rush of the asphalt beneath my wheels soothed me, to the extent where I almost forgot everything that was churning around deep in my troubled soul. Almost.

All too soon, however, my brief interlude of blissful ignorance came to an end as I saw the slip road, down which I would need to turn, come into view. The old, blue sign, still cheery and familiar despite the years, announced

'MOTORWAY SERVICES', printed in white, along with the familiar pictures, slightly faded, indicating that I could eat, sleep and have a shower there, should I so desire. The fuel picture, however, had been boldly and obviously crossed-out in thick, yellow ink or paint.

Using the same brush or pen, someone had scrawled 'open' in huge letters along the bottom of the sign, the yellow contrasting perfectly with the blue background. That wrung a little smile from my weary bones as I subconsciously fingered the tattered card in my pocket, thinking of her and hoping to find some of that warmth again, before my spirit completely froze. Then, up ahead, looming at the side of the carriageway, I saw my destination.

It looked exactly like any of the countless other abandoned motorway service areas that I had passed on my journey north, except that there was a large wall, made of assorted debris and burned-out vehicles, piled high, that protected the building housing the traveller facilities. To the left, outside the wall, was the fuel service station area, completely deserted and clearly roped off with red and white striped plastic tape, which I thought was a nice touch. I smiled to myself as I stood watching it flutter in the wind, announcing inconvenience to any would-be customers, just like the good old days.

Along the forecourt display, which had once thrust the oil company's name into the view of motorists on the road, had been scrawled 'NO FUEL LEFT' in huge letters. It looked to be written in the same medium as was used on the sign back on the motorway. Luckily, I was not there for gasoline.

I slowed as I approached the gate: two large sheets of corrugated metal riveted and welded into a fully functioning, and foreboding, entrance way, which was firmly closed. I suddenly felt a little unsure of how to proceed and stopped my bike before the entry, conscious of how exposed and defenceless I now was.

It was then that I noticed the guards stationed on the walls. They were all staring at me intently from their positions atop the barricade. As my eyes automatically zoomed and focused, I saw instantly that they all had large, and highly visible, firearms in their hands and looked highly trained and very alert. Their weapons, too, looked well-maintained and ready to be put to immediate use, if necessary.

I stood perfectly still, then lowered my bike gently to the floor and slowly straightened up, putting my hands in the air, very obviously, to show that I was unarmed and therefore not a threat. I still, as usual, had my trusty knife in my waistband but the guards did not need to know that and I certainly posed no danger to people with guns, standing beyond my reach. I was completely at their mercy.

As I was searching for the right words to defuse the palpable tension of the situation, I was taken off-guard by a sudden question.

"What's your business?" The male voice was firm, but the tone polite, educated, the like of which I had not heard for an age.

"I am a traveller and I seek refreshment," I replied, awkwardly, though I suddenly realised that I wasn't exactly sure what my business was. Honestly, I felt like a fool. There I was trying to sound cultured, and therefore definitely not like a barbarian from the outer wastelands, but I just ended up sounding archaic and ridiculous, to my ears at least.

"And what brings you here, traveller? So far from home?" A question again came from above. I had no idea if he had noticed my accent and was talking about my country of birth or if he merely meant the long journey that I'd made north, from my riverside hovel, to get there. Either way, honesty was certainly the best policy in the situation and, in both cases, my answer would be the same. There was only one reason for my being there.

"A friend told me about you. We always talked about coming here, together, one day," I explained and waved the tiny card high in the air, not even sure if the guards could see it but hoping it would distract from the pain that oozed through the feigned confidence of my words.

"Where is your friend now? They did not come?" Another question, but a little softer in tone.

"She passed before we were ready to make the trip. She died in childbirth," I said quickly, hoping to get the words out before they shattered in my mouth and drew fresh blood.

"That's a shame, we are sorry for your loss." The voice sounded a little warmer and the sentiment appeared to be genuine. I was a little taken aback, to say the least, and I merely stared, open-mouthed.

"Come in and be refreshed, then, traveller," boomed the guard, grandiosely. Either he, too, was now speaking archaically or he was just gently making fun of me. I could either smile along or I could get angry, then get shot, so I cracked a hesitant grin and managed a low chuckle, my first in months, even if it was forced. The entrance swung noisily open, and I cautiously wheeled my bicycle inside.

I came to a halt after I had cleared the gates, which were labouring shut behind me. Patiently, I waited while two of the guards descended from their vantage point and approached. They came to a stop, studying me intently from head to toe. No doubt they were looking for any signs that I was carrying the infection but, eventually, they seemed satisfied that I was not a threat. I sensed that the immediate danger had passed but I also noticed that, although they were relaxed and smiling, their guns remained trained firmly on me, just in case.

"Right, there are no weapons allowed in the compound, so put it slowly on the floor, please," the first guard ordered in an almost jovial tone.

I made an open-handed gesture and was about to say that I had nothing when the nearest guard explained, "He means that knife you have in your waistband."

I was too stunned to protest and meekly reached behind me, took out my trusty blade and laid it gently on the floor in front of me.

"We've been watching you for a while," the sentry explained, in answer to my unvoiced question. She then stepped forward and patted me down, searching for any other concealed weapons, stepping back when she was satisfied that I was completely unarmed.

"I see," I replied softly, still reeling in surprise. They had obviously been tracking me and I had had no idea.

"Can we see the business card?" the first sentry asked politely, interrupting my train of thought.

"Sure," I answered, pulling it out of my pocket and presenting it to them.

"One of the older ones but obviously, they're circulating," sentry number one said to his partner, looking pleased.

"Yeah," sentry number two nodded, "where did you say you came from, sir?" She turned back towards me, also smiling.

"Down near the capital but out in the sticks, downriver from the city," I told them, as vaguely as possible.

"That's a long way from here, and you came all this way on a *bicycle*?" The first guard looked surprised, and I even thought I detected a little admiration in his voice.

"Good to see our message is getting out, though. Where did your friend get it, do you know?" his colleague asked, gently.

"She said she found it clutched in the hand of a dead body, before she met me, but I'm not sure exactly where, sorry. That's all she told me."

Actually, she had told me she'd found it in the corpse's pocket, whilst checking for anything valuable, but I gave them the slightly more poetic version. I severely doubted that these people scavenged, by the looks of them; they even had clean fingernails.

"Well, I suppose you're thirsty and I'm sure you didn't come all this way just to talk to *us*. Follow the road ahead until you come to the main building. You can't miss it, it looks just like they used to."

The first sentry beamed a huge, genuine smile at me then raised his hand to indicate the way. I offered them my stuttering gratitude and bid them farewell as they set about remounting the walls. Once they had resumed their positions, I hopped on my bike and followed the road, past the well-maintained trees and bushes, towards the main building, shining in the near distance like a beacon.

The service area looked exactly like they did in the old days. The car park, empty apart from a small, truck-style vehicle, was clean and free of debris. The white lines looked fresh, as if they had been recently redone, though they were slightly uneven in places, like they had been done by hand.

I had passed many old, disused rest areas next to the motorways on my long voyage north, but they were nothing like this. The others had all been overgrown and crumbling, with no sign of life and no possible welcome to a civilised traveller, just horrors hidden, or hiding, within.

This site definitely seemed operational, not just an act, not merely for show, and the thought fanned the tiny ember that was starting to glow, once again, deep in my being. I was beginning to dare to hope that I had found what I had been looking for, what I'd been dreaming of all those long years: a refuge where civilisation stood tall and proud against the casual barbarity of this bleak, changed world.

The organisation of the place hinted at a social structure, and level of cooperation, that I had thought to no longer exist and the prospect filled me with an almost giddy sense of budding joy. That was tempered somewhat by the slight fear that it could be a trap, a ruse to lure hapless travellers to some horrific doom, but, after coming so far, struggling so long and leaving behind the only life I had known, I had nothing more to give and nothing left to lose, so on I pedalled.

I approached the main doors to the complex and immediately saw human activity. To the right was what looked like a restaurant, and, through the immaculately polished windows, I could see people walking around, serving themselves, greeting each other and eating at tables in groups, talking and laughing. I stood still, gawking inanely through the window at this scene.

I had to fight the urge to pinch my skin, as it all seemed like a dream, so boringly *normal*, but a kind of normality that I hadn't seen for almost a decade and had feared was no longer possible. To the left of the restaurant, on the other side of the doors, again with spotlessly clean windows, was a café, one of those lounge-style coffee bars that could, once upon a time, have been seen anywhere in the world, with comfortable furniture and generic pictures on the walls.

There were people sitting, drinking and talking in the chairs and others ordering drinks at the bar. I could see the staff behind the counter, wearing pristine green aprons and black garments underneath. The whole image was achingly familiar and I suddenly realised just how much I had missed the trivial, banal minutiae of an existence I had once considered excruciatingly mundane.

I trembled as I caught sight of my reflection, looking in the window. I finally understood how incredibly lonely I had been, for most of my desolate existence, since the breakdown of society made me the pitiful wretch that I saw now, staring back at me in the glass, with hollow eyes sunk deep in a gaunt and ravaged face. The epiphany was powerful, and I stood there for what seemed like long minutes while I regained my composure. A few people within noticed me and waved, smiling, and that snapped me back to reality, very self-consciously.

I parked my bike in the designated 'bicycle parking' area, which was otherwise empty. The lines looked quite fresh and I wondered, idly, if they'd painted them especially for me. I left my trusty, two-wheeled vehicle carefully leaning against the railing; I didn't have a lock but I very much doubted that I would need one, anyway.

I took a deep breath as I stepped up to the sliding doors and was a little surprised, even disappointed, when they didn't open automatically as I had half-expected. Instead, I stood, looking confused and peering up at the sensors, until someone inside hurried over and slid the doors open, manually, for me. I remained there for a second, openly staring in amazement at the young lady who stood before me. She was cleanly dressed, and her hair was washed, brushed and fragrant. The contrast between the two of us, caught for a brief second in a pastiche of awkwardness, could not have been greater. I reeked of death and long weeks of neglect, while she was a radiant, wholesome vision from our considerably more hygienic history.

At that moment, I heard a cry of 'Mummy, Mummy!' then two young children, a boy and a girl: also immaculately dressed, came cannoning out of the restaurant and smothered their mother in cuddles and kisses, before they each began shouting, at the same time, of how the other had so grievously wronged them and, of course, loudly proclaiming their respective innocence. I smiled briefly and managed to mumble, "Thanks," before looking down at my feet.

"You're welcome," she replied with an easy smile, displaying her white, well-maintained teeth, not quite 'Hollywood Pearly' but most definitely *not* 'Apocalypse Black'. Then, she turned her attention to her flailing children and led them off back into the restaurant, without looking back. I was left standing timidly in the entrance, not really sure what to do.

I looked across to the restaurant and a staff-member waved and beckoned me in as I stood staring at the mother and her children, settling down once more at a large table away from the windows. I waved back but I wasn't really hungry, so I smiled an apology, turned towards the café and put my hand on the door.

Before going in, I hesitated as I took a long and critical look down at my appearance. I was very conscious of the fact that everyone else I had seen was well-dressed, clean and presentable. They did not look like they had been sleeping rough for weeks, in the same clothes, as I obviously did and, in fact, had been. I was dirty, shabby, ill-shaven and, above all, I stank.

The odour was eye-watering, even to me, so I could only imagine how bad it would be to others, especially if they were used to the considerably more delicately perfumed denizens of their world. I had not felt so self-conscious for a long, long while and I realised that I must look, and smell, like a complete savage.

A sickening fear struck me: did I appear to them as the very epitome of everything *I* professed to despise in humanity? I lifted my eyes from studying my filthy hands and grimy fingernails to see that a man was now standing before me, holding the door open and dressed in the familiar green apron of someone who worked in the café.

"It's okay," he said, with a gentle smile, "come in and sit down."

"But I'm filthy. I am ashamed," I entreated, eyes brimming with horror and my chagrin clear.

"That's no problem, you've been travelling a long while, we know, and we all looked like you when we arrived, too. I wasn't wearing a shirt and tie when *I* got here, believe me." He took my arm, lightly, and led me towards the counter.

"But I have no money, I cannot buy anything," I again protested. He merely laughed, but not unkindly.

"Don't worry, that's one aspect of the old world that we choose not to keep. Now, what would you like to drink?"

I looked up at the menu, handwritten and worn, and was spoiled for choice. For long years, I had dreamed of hot cups of coffee, with real, full-fat milk and brown sugar. The instant stuff, cooked in an old tin over a fire with powdered milk and processed sugar (that would not spoil), did not even begin to satisfy that fantasy.

"I'd love a latte, please," I decided eventually, my shame momentarily forgotten.

"Okay, sir, if you'd like to sit down, I'll bring it across when it's ready."

"Thanks," I gushed and headed for a seat by the window, away from everyone else.

As I passed the few tables that held occupants, they all looked up, smiled and offered me a greeting, to which I mumbled a reply. My embarrassment returned fully to the fore. I felt too ashamed to look them in the face; these people who were, so obviously, everything that I was not but yet everything that I had, until my arrival, considered myself to be. The role reversal was almost too much to bear, and I sank silently down into my chair, staring fixedly out of the window to avoid making eye contact with anyone.

Through the panes, I could see the disused service station off to the right and the wall of the compound directly ahead of me. Interestingly, despite its obvious defensive strength, the palisade was not very high. In the background, I could see a small road as it snaked away, pristine and barren, up the mountainside, until even my enhanced eyes could no longer follow it.

The surrounding area was lush and green, contrasting sharply with the dull, grey clouds overhead. It, too, seemed as deserted as the tiny mountain road. I could see no signs of life in the immediate vicinity, apart from what was on the compound itself.

The vista was starkly beautiful, but its emptiness only served to accentuate my feelings of loneliness and exclusion. There was nothing out there and there seemed to be nothing for me here, either. I had lost everything, sacrificing even the meagre life that I had built, and now it looked as if I had found nothing, too. Loneliness was far easier to bear when one was not surrounded by strangers, so clearly enjoying each other's company.

I looked away from the window and turned my attention to the coffee that had appeared before me, which certainly looked authentic. It even came in a roughly made paper cup with a strange, mermaid-type thing drawn on it in green pen. I'd never really known what it represented anyway so, even though it wasn't exactly right, it was certainly good enough.

I closed my eyes in anticipation and raised the steaming cup to my mouth, taking a large gulp despite the handwritten 'extremely hot' warning on the cup. There was no mistaking the taste, that was a real coffee and I let out a satisfied sigh as I swallowed a mouthful.

I reverently savoured each drop and sensation as I sipped, slowly yet steadily. I then placed the half-empty cup back on the table and was a little embarrassed to notice that a few people were looking at me and smiling as I, very noticeably, enjoyed my drink. I went bright red beneath the caked-on mask of grime that used to be my face and reached into my filthy travelling bag to quickly pull out something to read.

Books were one relic of the old society that could still be enjoyed in its aftermath. They needed no electricity nor fuel and they could be carried and read anywhere one wished. It amazed me to think that once, we carried entire libraries in hand-held devices but now, many years later, a simple book, made of paper and ink, was one of the few usable remnants of a technological society that would, most probably, never exist again. More practically, they also brought me much solace.

I sensed someone next to me and glanced sideways to see the server was standing nearby, waiting patiently for me to notice his presence. When I looked up, he smiled patiently and indicated what I was reading.

"If you like, when you finish that, you can swap it for another one, over there," he said, gesturing with his left hand towards a large, full bookcase to the right of the counter.

"Thank you," I answered and tried to return his effortlessly warm smile, but it had been so long that I wasn't sure it came across as intended, so I self-consciously looked back down at my novel. He lingered without replying for a second, until I looked up and smiled again, a little more confidently and successfully this time. I was about to ask him if there was anything else when he spoke.

"Actually," he offered, "when you've finished your coffee, if you don't mind, the manager would like to have a word with you."

"Okay, uh…what about?" I asked, suddenly a little worried.

"I'm not sure," he said, raising his eyebrows and giving me an enigmatic smile that suggested he knew exactly what the boss wanted to see me about. "Just come across when you're ready, no rush." He then turned and went back to his station, behind the counter.

I realised that something important was about to happen and, not wanting to hang around anymore, I drained my latte and replaced it on the table. I then stood up and made my way across for the meeting, dropping my empty cup in one of the period-accurate black bin bags on the way.

As I approached the bar, a lady came from behind a swing door the other side and smiled broadly at me. She walked around to the customer side of the counter and offered me her hand as she introduced herself as the manager of the café, whatever that meant. I grasped her palm in a tentative shake and introduced myself, though it felt extremely strange to hear her repeat my name: she was only the second person in many years.

She turned and then led me into a small room, through the same door by which she had entered. She gestured for me to sit down at a table in the centre of the space and I acquiesced wordlessly. I noticed various personal effects scattered around the edges of the room: coats on hooks and muddy boots on racks beneath them and I realised that it must be some kind of employee area.

Things were starting to become bewilderingly surreal, and I was not really sure how to act, although I had not felt in any danger since arriving at this strange place. I was even beginning to relax a little, softened by the unexpected kindness and generosity I had, thus far, experienced. I was not totally sure, but it seemed that the trauma from the harsh reality of my recent life and the nightmare of my desperate journey to get there was already starting to recede. I also considered the fact that it could merely be the coffee coursing through my system, blissfully altering my sensory perception. Either way, it was a very welcome feeling and a genuine, unforced grin suddenly broke free and spread across my face.

The Manager then sat down opposite me and returned my smile. She seemed to be waiting for me to talk, though I did not really know what to say and I started to feel a little awkward.

"Is it about my bill? I left my wallet at home," I joked, trying to break the ice.

"No," she chuckled, "but if you would like to give something in return for our hospitality, then I have a proposition for you."

"What's that?" I asked, intrigued by her sudden earnestness. The conversation was friendly but very serious, that much I could fathom. Just then, we were interrupted by the server bringing in two fresh cups of coffee for us.

"Well, we are always looking for people to work and help us out with our life here," The Manager continued.

"Um…I don't really know anything about working in a café, sorry."

"That's not exactly what I meant. We usually ask people to contribute by doing something related to what they used to do, to use their old skills. What *did* you do, you know, before?" she asked, softly.

"I was a teacher," I replied carefully, "primary school." The memories seemed incredibly remote and it was a real effort to collect them into any sort of meaningful cohesion.

"Excellent, we could use another teacher for our children. Would you like to stay?"

I started to reply, caught off-guard by her sudden directness, but she cut me off.

"Don't answer straight away. Let me give you a tour of our setup, then you can decide later."

She stood up, smiled, and gestured towards the door. I would not even have dreamed of saying no, so I, too, rose and followed her out.

I walked by her side as she showed me all around the deceptively large compound. Everywhere we went, residents stopped to wave, smile and say hello. They gladly took time out of their busy days to enquire politely after my journey and general well-being.

I saw nothing but happiness and industriousness; there was no violence, no aggression in the air at all, no danger. There were armed guards surveying the inhabitants as they worked, for sure, but they were so obviously there to defend, not to attack. The constant threat of mortal danger, which had permeated my entire solitary existence, seemed so distant, so remote that the guards even took the time to talk and joke with us as we walked by.

I saw fields stretching away behind the buildings, high up into the mountains, where crops were grown and animals grazed, to provide food for all. People were working, taking part everywhere we went, and children played among them: happy, safe and smiling.

My guide told me how they all contributed what they could for the community's needs, whether that be harvesting, cooking, working in her café or something else. She explained that everyone took on a role when they arrived, based on what they had done before, to ensure that old skills survived and were nurtured. This system also encouraged new talents to emerge and develop. Each person's contribution was valued and, more importantly, valued equally. She was only manager, she insisted, because she had previous experience and she would not be allowed to stay in the role indefinitely.

I was then introduced to a man who had just arrived, a few weeks earlier, and was a former electrician. He told me how he was working on designing and building a system to generate enough power for the whole compound. The manager joked that then, I'd be able to use the automatic doors and we all joined in with her laughter, warm and real.

On the way back, I told her that I'd had my eyes surgically enhanced and she suggested, in a serious tone, that I could maybe do some lookout duty, too, to watch out for those who would seek to destroy what they had created and take it for themselves. As I suspected, though, she told me there were no longer many of them left in the area, thanks to the frequent patrols. As to whether the patrols somehow dissuaded encroachers or simply eliminated them, she did not elaborate, and I did not ask. I did not want, or even really care, to know.

Eventually, we found ourselves back in the employees' room of the café, cradling another steaming cup of coffee and looking at each other across the table.

"Well," I began, with a last prick of that old caution, "do you give everyone the same tour?"

"More or less," she said, smiling, not seeming at all surprised by my question, "and they all say yes."

"I see," I replied, carefully, attempting to sound as neutral as possible. She did not appear to have heard as she suddenly stood up and opened one of the lockers to her left.

"Wait, before you decide, one more thing. Here are some fresh, clean clothes and here is a towel. Head out of the café, take a left and the shower and toilet block is in front of you. Go and clean yourself up and then we'll meet back here to talk. Oh, and take your time. Enjoy it. Nobody is going anywhere."

I took the bundle from her eagerly and almost ran in the direction she had indicated, excited to finally be able to get out of my stinking rags: out of my visible, obvious shame, and clean myself up.

I reached the door to the toilet area and it swung effortlessly open at my touch. I was amazed to find myself standing in a sparkling, clean bathroom, with urinals, showers, handbasins and glittering silver taps, resplendent in their shining, bone-white and chrome glory.

I walked slowly over to the sink area, like a child entranced by a new toy, and turned one of the taps on. Water came flowing out, cool at first but then, to my delight, it became soothingly warm: not too hot, just right.

I kept my hands under the stream for a few minutes, turning them over and over, with undisguised glee, before I put them under the soap dispenser and pumped the button. Green gel dribbled slowly into my outstretched palms, and I rushed them back under the warm tap. In amazement, I watched the layers of filth begin to come away as I rubbed the soap into my skin under the hot water. I looked over to the cubicles and, when I saw the working toilets within, I ran across to relieve myself, even though it was unnecessary. I even sat down to urinate, just because I could.

When I had finished, I took a rough tissue: authentic to the last detail, from the dispenser and then flushed the chain, watching in amazement as the water rolled and surged away, sucking down the dirty liquid and paper, then seeping in again to slowly and steadily refill the bowl. These were all things that I had once taken for granted but they now seemed as breathtaking as magic tricks to an uninitiated child.

Finally, I took a long shower, scrubbing away the entrenched layers of dirt and grime from every inch of my body until I stood, naked, cleansed and glowing, under the soothing, tepid flow.

Eventually, I stepped out, drying myself methodically with the fresh towel. Then, I got dressed in the clothes I had been given: blue jeans, a plain t-shirt and a thick jumper, with a pair of sturdy socks and boots. They would certainly not have been called stylish in prior times but they more or less fitted and they were warm, which was more than good enough for me.

At last, I looked clean and ready to become a member of a civilised society once more. I emerged from the facilities area and walked confidently back into the main hallway of the building. There was a new spring in my step and I held my head high, as I finally looked and felt like someone who belonged.

It was beginning to grow dark outside and plastic-covered lamps now lit the interior of the building, fixed to the ceiling and walls. As I walked past a light fitting, I noticed it flicker slightly and stood on my tiptoes to look inside. I saw that it was filled with small candles and remembered what I'd been told about there not being enough electricity for the whole compound. The candles had the desired effect, however, as the whole building was filled with soft lighting. It was also a subtle reminder that the whole place was only a recreation of what had once existed and not quite the real thing: not yet, at least.

As I padded in the direction of the food court, I noticed that although there were people about, they were different to those who had been there when I had first arrived. I walked into the café and the manager was already sitting at a table as if waiting for me, which she probably was. She motioned for me to sit down, with her.

"You look like a different person," she beamed at me, "though you didn't have a shave. Still, the beard kind of suits you, you know. Very modern, very dystopian-chic." She gave me a flirtatious wink.

"Thanks," I said, running my hand self-consciously over the thick, untameable growth on my face, "maybe tomorrow." I smiled sheepishly.

"Great! Well, we've prepared a room for you in the hotel. You'll be on your own to start with, of course, but if you find someone you'd like to share with in the future, you can always move." She looked suddenly coy. Then, a slight shadow of doubt fell upon her face. "You will stay with us, won't you?" she asked earnestly, seeming a little unsure.

I looked around at the clean, warm, smiling faces, I felt the cup of hot coffee in my hand and I thought of my hole in the ground, far away by some forgotten river. I considered all the horrors I'd seen and grimaced internally at the memory of the dreadful sins I'd committed, just to survive. I reflected on everything I'd lost and wondered if I could somehow make it all *matter*. I considered the hope I could sense entwined in the very fabric of this place, in these people. I weighed a possible future *life* against a future of merely existing until my premature death and I realised, there was no choice to make.

I exhaled slowly and said, "Yes."

City

I woke from another nightmare, drenched with sweat, and reached, out of habit, for the bottle next to my bed that was no longer there. I closed my eyes, but I could still see the horror, vividly burned into my consciousness.

Images of screaming, blood-filled mouths and dying children, whispering insistent accusations, returned as soon as my eyelids, heavy with sleep, tried to sneak themselves closed. I forced them to remain open and sat, shivering, for a long while, trying to will the bad visions from my mind and hopefully get some sleep before teaching in the morning. I knew I was only dreaming but how can you prevent the things that you have seen haunting you, when the night closes in and sleep allows your subconscious mind to roam freely and remind you of who you truly are?

***

As soon as it became clear that things were too far gone to salvage, I realised that I needed to get out of town: immediately. Events were rapidly going from bad to worse as society began to implode messily, eating itself from within, but I knew I had a much better chance of survival if I could just escape to the countryside.

I needed to get away from the human filth filling the city, the pestilence spreading like wildfire through the population and the growing danger on the streets as law and order slowly collapsed. People were suddenly experiencing a new kind of liberty and the results were getting uglier, and increasingly savage, with each passing day.

I decided to fill a rucksack with some dried food, water, a torch, spare clothes and a first-aid kit. I also packed a large, half-empty bottle of sanitiser: all I had to hand, and some disposable face masks. It was not much but the contents were light and would, hopefully, keep me alive long enough to make my escape to a rural haven.

I looked long and hard at the knives resting on the kitchen surface, weighing the potential need for a weapon against my reluctance to use one, before tucking a small blade into my waistband, behind my back, and pulling my shirt down to conceal it as best as possible. I might need to be armed to protect myself, but I definitely did not want to look like an aggressor, for reasons that were not merely to do with safety but also my code of ethics.

Despite those noble principles, a tiny part of me wished that I had more than just a knife. I could really have used something more potent against the mobs that were becoming increasingly frequent, though mainly in the less salubrious areas of town, it had to be said.

I desperately needed to get out of the city, but I had a crucial journey to make first, which was why I was up so unnaturally early. The electricity had cut out completely, and finally, during the night and had not come back on. With no way of receiving news or updates on the situation and no sign of the power returning, I knew that things had reached a critical juncture.

The energy supply had gone down before but never for so long and there had always been cars in the street blaring updates and preaching calm, until then. Even the incessant sirens and gunfire, which had become a ubiquitous soundtrack to the last few weeks, had seemingly vanished.

That morning, the silence was ominous and the atmosphere in the city had palpably changed; I could tell that just by sticking my head out of the window. I felt a nagging knot in the pit of my stomach and needed to go and check on my friend before leaving. I hoped I'd be able to convince her to come with me.

She'd said she was feeling very tired when we had parted last night and had wanted to go home, rather than stay at mine. We'd only just made it back to her place before curfew, so I had wanted to stay with her, but she had insisted that I return to my home to protect it from looters on the prowl. Once darkness fell, the streets soon filled with opportunistic scavengers, looking for easier pickings in a nicer part of town, and she was concerned that they might target my building, too.

With hindsight, I should have insisted on staying, but I'd given in to her stubbornness and had jogged the short distance back home to my apartment. I deeply regretted it now, with the recent developments, but, to my shame, I had been thinking of my new kitchen, with all the latest gadgets, that I had bought only a month earlier, before everything had started to fall apart. It had cost me almost a month's salary and I had foolishly thought that something worth protecting. As I stood there in the blinding clarity of the early morning sun, a little fear set in, and I very much doubted the merit in my decision to return home alone.

I had woken at first light, worried, and decided to hurry across to her place as quickly as possible, before most people were up and about their day, however they chose to spend it. It was not a great plan, but it was the best I could do for now. I just hoped it wasn't too late.

I stepped out into the street warily and immediately raised my hand to shield my eyes. Though it was barely daylight, the sun's rays beat heavily down on my bare neck and head and its intensity was already blinding.

It should have been a day for sitting outside: eating, drinking and enjoying the early summer weather. Instead, the unusually warm conditions had facilitated the rapid spread of the virus and exacerbated the condition of the streets, with stinking rubbish piles and excrement filling the city at an alarming rate. The stench was aggressive, and I was in a more prosperous area, heaven only knew what it was like elsewhere.

The boulevards were mercifully empty at that time of the morning, almost as if everyone was actually sticking to the stay-at-home orders that were, seemingly, revised on a daily basis. I moved swiftly, striding purposefully down the centre of the road; there was no need to worry about cars anymore as fuel was rarer than fresh food.

It was not that far to her place from mine, and I quickly covered the distance. As I drew nearer, however, I became aware of a growing hubbub in the distance and slowed down a little; surely there could not be a mob forming already that early in the morning? I was still in the 'safe' part of town, although it did border a slightly riskier district and the definition of 'safe' had undergone serious revision of late.

I warily rounded the corner to the side street that contained her apartment block and was greeted by a large throng of people, gathered outside the front entrance to her place and stretching ten metres or so on either side. Not one member of the assembled crowd appeared to be taking any precautions against the virus: no masks, no personal space, but I was hardly surprised. The building's doors themselves were cordoned off with huge, portable barriers that carried prominent 'no entry' and 'biohazard' warnings in lurid yellow, black and red. Despite this clear reminder of the danger, nobody seemed to care as they jostled each other for a better view.

Parked haphazardly in front, with sirens flashing but silent and its doors flung wide open, stood a medical van, flanked by a jeep-style military transport in its pale urban camouflage. There were obvious stains of dried red on the bonnets of both vehicles, along with fresh scratches and what looked like bullet holes along their flanks.

Standing, impassive and silent in front of the vehicles, intermittently scanning the crowd on all sides and watching the doors, were two heavily armed soldiers in full battle fatigues, carrying the insignia and wearing the headgear of an elite regiment. Even their medical-grade facemasks bore the unit's crest and colours, which I thought was a nice touch, especially in such desperate times.

As I hung back, craning my neck to get the best possible view of the situation whilst remaining at a safe distance from my fellow onlookers, a young, shirtless man covered in lurid, patriotic tattoos, who was standing near me, caught my gaze and explained.

"They've quarantined the building, no one is allowed in or out. They're gonna *purge* 'em."

I just nodded, not really taking in what he had said. I was more concerned with trying to find a safe way to get around the rabble and closer to her building but to no avail, the crowd was too deep and too tightly packed. Then, between the heads of the throng in front, I saw a doctor dressed in a protective, anti-virus suit walk out from the main doors and head over to the elder of the two servicemen. He looked directly at the officer, removed his helmet and, almost imperceptibly, shook his masked head.

The uniformed men instantly sprang to work. The younger trooper began barking orders at the crowd as he advanced towards them, firing shots into the air. The onlookers were ordered to disperse, for their own safety, while the senior soldier marched purposefully over to the medical vehicle to pick up some protective headgear. He jammed it over his face as he strode into the now-open doors of the apartment block, slinging his weapon into a firing position as he moved.

Despite the heat of the day, I felt a chill run through the core of my being as I watched, powerless to do anything or to even find out what was happening. People began to fall back slightly at the sound of the gunshots but voyeuristic instinct kept most of them there, to observe events as they unfolded.

Some of the onlookers no doubt lived in the area, maybe even in the building itself, but human nature dictated that most would be there simply to watch, driven by a morbid curiosity, with some even deriving pleasure from the misfortune of others. However, in their possible defence, as non-essential services were all shuttered, there was precious little else available in terms of entertainment, so their curiosity was somewhat understandable.

I took advantage of the retreating crowd to move around and further forwards, until I was pushing at the barrier that cordoned off the front of the entranceway, but still at a safe distance from my fellow citizens. Standing on the other side of the metal barricade, with his gun at the ready, was the younger soldier. Two more medical staff then appeared out of the apartment building but even their heavy masks could not fully conceal the troubled looks on their faces and their anxious body language. I attempted to lean across and ask the trooper what was happening but was shoved roughly backwards, for my troubles, by an arm seemingly forged of steel. It was all I could do to maintain my balance.

The crowd suddenly hushed, as what sounded like muffled shots echoed from deep within the building. Then, the senior soldier emerged, with his face set in a grim expression behind the visor. He gave a brief, indiscernible signal to the medical team before removing his headgear, tossing it onto the floor and hastily climbing into the back of the military vehicle. He immediately re-emerged holding a square control panel and gestured sharply at his subordinate with a hand chopping through the air.

"For your own safety, everybody get back, *now!*" shouted the junior trooper, again firing into the air. Upon seeing the medical team jump into their transport and start to back away from the building, people suddenly began to comply and I found myself virtually the only person remaining at the front of the barrier.

I briefly caught the eye of the younger soldier, keeping my distance this time, and began to form an urgent question but he cut me off with a barked command to 'back away' and body language that thoroughly convinced me of the seriousness of the situation. When the two soldiers themselves jumped into their vehicle, which then started to roll ominously backwards, I finally relented and retreated about five metres, until I was equidistant between the barrier and the fearful onlookers.

As I struggled to see what was happening inside the vehicles, I thought I saw the officer engage the control panel in his hand and, with no hesitation, firmly press it down. Without a sound, the whole building imploded, falling in upon itself and sending out a blast of aftershock that lifted me off my feet and threw me, hard, to the floor a few metres back.

With a shake of my head, I rose gingerly to my feet, relieved that nothing seemed injured, and looked around bewilderedly for the apartment block. It was completely gone, leaving nothing but a faint impression on the ground of where it had once stood and a few thick piles of dust, stirring gently in the morning breeze. The adjoining tenements were untouched and perfectly intact but sporting dark shadows, showing where the destroyed building had stood against them.

The crowd was stunned into silence at this awesome display of power but I reacted quickly, driven by sheer panic and terror. I ran forward, back to the barrier, and waved to attract the soldiers' attention as they emerged from their blast-proof vehicle and resumed their position, eyeing the mob. I caught the younger one's eye and shouted at him, removing my mask a little to make my words clearer.

"What the hell was that?"

He didn't answer, he just looked at me, steely eyed, and unshouldered his weapon.

"What about the people who lived there?" I tried again, frantically, but he just shrugged his shoulders, almost imperceptibly, and fixed his gaze at a point beyond me. Then, I saw his eyes widen as he watched the crowd behind.

I turned and immediately realised that everyone in the crowd was now staring at me in silence: some in fear and some in anger. The shirtless young man who had spoken to me earlier, as an equal and a fellow human being, had stepped forward slightly, ahead of the rest, with his finger extended towards me, accusingly.

"He's a foreigner, they brought the disease here and they are the ones spreading it!" he shouted.

Though he was merely repeating, parrot-fashion, what certain populist aspects of the media had been saying in recent weeks, I could still see, by the fervent look in their eyes and their suddenly aggressive stances, that a large section of the crowd was in agreement. A different man stepped forward.

"Cull them, stop the spread, save our children."

Another gem of a slogan from the nation's greatest political thinkers and, though it was hardly an original sentiment in the history of our species, many in the crowd began to cheer as if this were some fresh slice of genius and started to repeat it, like a ghastly mantra.

The shirtless man, evidently the bravest, or maybe just the most brainwashed, began to pace menacingly towards me, with murder shining, demon-bright, in his eyes. As a handful of men began to follow their new puppeteer, I realised that the situation was about to escalate horribly, for me, and an almost-incapacitating fear gripped hold of my entire being.

All of a sudden, it seemed that the virus was the least of my concerns.

I turned back to the barrier and looked to the soldier for assistance but he just stared, empty-eyed and impassive, at the scene unfolding before him. Perhaps he had his orders, or possibly, he sympathised with the belligerent savages behind me. In either case, I would get no help from him.

I cursed him through clenched teeth, questioning whether or not he had been born in wedlock, but still received no reaction. I looked around me wildly for the briefest of moments, in near panic, then my thought process came to an abrupt stop as the adrenaline kicked in.

I quickly vaulted the barrier and broke into a sudden run, catching even the watchful soldier by surprise. A section of the crowd followed suit, led on by the shirtless man, who effortlessly cleared the barricade and broke into a steady jog to match my own. The two soldiers made no attempt to stop them and allowed my pursuers to stream by, heading straight for me.

I was almost one hundred percent sure that I was running for my life, but I still felt a familiar tingle of wounded pride. It galled me, having to run from such people. It stung to have to bow to their unreasoning, violent hatred but I could not fight them all and I clearly risked getting more than just a beating: much, much more.

Tempering my prideful resentment with the clarity of common sense, I had no doubt that I was now being hunted by a rabid lynch mob. My only viable concern, therefore, was getting away, getting to safety. Increasing my speed, I started to sprint down the street, with no clue as to where I was going, I just needed to watch the ground beneath me in order to make sure I didn't trip or stumble. Were I to fall, my life story would quickly move on to its finale, ending prematurely as a tragedy of epic proportions, for me, at least.

I dared a quick look, back over my shoulder, and saw that I'd left most of my pursuers behind, apart from the shirtless man, who was younger and significantly less corpulent than most comprising the mobs. In fact, he appeared to be gaining on me, ever so slightly. I was now flat out, moving as fast as I could, and he was still catching me, so I changed tactics and turned into the next side alley in the hope of losing him. To my horror, however, I realised that I had ducked down a dead end when I came to a sudden stop in front of a high wall, which was blocking me from a sure escape.

There was nowhere to hide, and it was much too late to run back out onto the street. I briefly felt very afraid, as the full reality of my situation sank in, but I reacted quickly, deciding to use the one advantage I had in this scenario: my brain.

First, I selected a large chunk of rubble from the floor and, gripping the fingers of my right hand around it, held it out of sight behind my back. I then forced my face into a mask of the purest fear I could muster, which was not difficult at all given the predicament I was in.

As I swivelled to face the street again, my pursuer turned the corner into the alley then slowed to a sinister, measured walk when he saw me cowering, trapped against the far wall. He advanced towards me, clearly enjoying the power, a vicious grin splitting his youthful face from ear to ear. As he approached, I thought about the knife in my waistband, but I was reluctant to use it unless absolutely necessary.

"Time to clean up some filth," he spat at me then laughed: an evil cackle. Evidently, he found his own statement witty, even if no one else would.

He reached into his back pocket and pulled out something that glittered in the morning sun as he thumbed it: a knife. That forced me to change my original plan from escape to attack and I regretted not unsheathing my own weapon. I flooded my face with more fear, most of it real, and even managed to whimper a plaintive 'please' as he approached close enough to strike. In spite of my terror, I still remembered to check for any visible signs of infection on my assailant but, thankfully, saw none.

He stopped for a brief second, fingering his blade, his eyes filling with a savage relish as he savoured an easy kill and enjoyed my distress. That was the half-chance that I needed, and I took it. I whipped my hand around from behind my back, straightening it as I released the piece of rubble at the last moment, aiming squarely for his head.

At that range, I could not miss, and the lump of rock caught the man directly under the nose with a solid, sickening crunch. He howled in pain and surprise as he clasped his hands to the wound, dropping the knife at his feet in the process and staggering backwards.

I sprang at once, stooping to pick up the fallen blade and, in a smooth motion, buried it deep in his unprotected abdomen, thrusting upwards. He gave another cry, though this one was muted by the hands covering his mouth, and then clutched at his gut, feebly. With his head wounds now visible, I was able to see the bloodied mess: torn skin and crushed bone, that my rock had made of his face.

He sank to his knees, defenceless and no longer a threat, sobs of pain bubbling through ruined lips. As I manoeuvred around him to escape, I saw his eyes fix on me, accusing and entreating in equal measure. Then, he toppled over, face down, into the dust. I did not look back as I hurriedly left the alley. I did not dare to.

Emerging into the bright sunshine of the main street, I realised that I could feel something sticky and wet between my fingers. I glanced down and saw, to my horror, that my hands and sleeves were covered in blood. I pulled up in shock. I could not walk down the street like that, covered in the residue of another man's life. What few police remained would surely arrest or even shoot me if I were seen roaming around in such a state.

I ducked back into the mouth of the alley and hurriedly pulled off my jacket in the shelter the side street afforded me. I was loath to use any precious sanitiser, so I used the inside of the coat to wipe off my hands and trousers as best I could, before slinging the garment disgustedly away in an instinctive reaction.

As I overcame my initial revulsion and bent down to hide the jacket properly behind a pile of refuse, conveniently located just inside the alley's entrance, I heard a faint groan coming from within. A wave of instant nausea swept across me as the realisation of what I had just done began to sink in.

I was now, for the first time in my life, a killer. I was a murderer. Whether it had been necessary, or not, was irrelevant, that did not change reality and the reality was that I had ended another's life. Clearly, my attacker was unlikely to survive his wounds, even if he were still alive for the time being.

Mercifully, this devastating epiphany lasted only a short second. I quickly remembered that I did not have the time to dwell on my actions just yet, so I forced those feelings to the back of my mind, shaking my head clear, as I realised the urgent need to focus on the present and press on with my attempted escape.

I briefly considered going back to her apartment building, but I knew in my heart of hearts that she was gone, atomised. If only I had come earlier, or stayed with her last night, events could have turned out differently. As things stood, though, I had to be ruthless if I wanted to survive. In all honesty, I knew there was nothing I could do now, or could have done earlier on, with the soldiers and the mob I would, no doubt, already be dead, but the guilt still twisted in my guts as I steeled myself for the next part of my journey.

When I emerged again into the light of the street, after hastily concealing my jacket, I immediately saw, and heard, a large, angry mob. It was making its way towards my position, surging up the boulevard that I was standing on, coming from the direction of the more dangerous part of town. I fell back, yet again, into the thrice-cursed alley, closing my ears to anything I might hear from inside to torment me, like furies, and concealed myself behind the large pile of stinking rubbish where I had stashed my jacket.

Averting my gaze from the silent reproach of my bloodstained garment, I manoeuvred so that I could watch as the mob stormed past. There were people of all ages and walks of life, some shouting for food, some shouting for salvation and some who seemed to be just shouting for the sake of it, all with their eyes glazed over in a fanatical fervour. They could well have been my pursuers from the same mob that I had seen before, heading back to re-join the others. They might even have been still looking for me. At any rate, I knew that I had to remain hidden from sight.

As they trudged past, a mindless, seething mass of bodies and noise, I could not for the life of me work out who they were shouting at. Who did they think would help? Who did they think would listen? Society was very obviously dying and perhaps we all realised that to be proactive meant a chance at survival, whereas passivity would ensure death. I just could not see what the lost souls marching by, so ardently, hoped to achieve.

After they had passed, I breathed a sigh of relief and relaxed, allowing a little mental clarity to reappear. As soon as the adrenaline started to wear off, however, my guilt instantly returned, like a hammer blow, and led me to follow the mob, albeit at a distance and carefully sticking to the safety of the shadows, as it made its way down the road, back towards my friend's apartment. I had to know, for sure, exactly what had happened to her.

When we reached her section of the street, I jumped stealthily onto a pile of rubble in order to get a clearer view of what was happening ahead of me. The soldiers and the medical vehicle remained outside but I saw instantly that several more buildings along the row had been atomised. There was still a sizeable crowd on the other side of the barriers, but the two troopers seemed to have them contained and controlled, at least for the moment.

The servicemen were not prepared, however, for the new arrivals, who had them flanked. On hearing their shouting, the junior soldier looked around and noticed the new rabble. He hurriedly turned to bark a clipped warning to his officer, who spoke back without turning his body and gave a command with a sharp chop of the hand. The chants and cries of the freshly arrived crowd carried to those kindred spirits in the other gathering and they suddenly sprang to life. Like sheep in adjacent fields, they, too, took up the calls and responses of mindless anger.

There was a moment of heavy expectation as the two mobs locked eyes with the soldiers, neither side moving. I saw a flash of white in the windows of the hospital van and realised that the medics must be hiding in there, attempting to shelter.

The tension was unbearable, and I was considering retreating to a safer place myself when the crowd on my side of the barrier, less than a hundred metres away, began to chant even more loudly. Then, someone threw a stone at the younger soldier. Although it missed by a wide margin, it was quickly followed by another, then a bottle that struck him a glancing blow on the shoulder. I could see beads of sweat forming on his face, and he fired into the air as the mob on my side began to move, menacingly, towards the hopelessly outnumbered troopers. In tandem, the mob on the other side of the barrier started to shuffle forward and the officer, too, let off a warning shot, shouting at the masses to get back.

All of a sudden, someone threw an improvised grenade, which landed at the feet of the young trooper, briefly setting his boots alight and he struggled to put them out without losing his grip on his weapon. Although he was not injured, something in the air changed, palpably, at that precise moment. Perhaps the rabble suddenly realised the extent of the soldiers' vulnerability, or maybe it just smelt blood.

The shouting intensified as both segments of the mob started jeering at the soldiers and brandishing makeshift weapons. A small band of stick-wielding men burst from the front of the group nearest me and charged the younger soldier, whooping like chimpanzees on the hunt.

The trooper shouted a warning and when this was ignored, he opened fire, bringing the men down, writhing, in a hail of automatic weapon shots. They lay, dead or dying, on the floor as their blood flowed out, intermingling and staining the cobbles of the street a deep, coagulating crimson.

That was the catalyst needed to finally provoke the rabble into violence and the crowd, on both sides, broke en masse and rushed the two soldiers. Scores fell in a hail of gunfire as they closed the gap into striking range, but the bullets did not slow the charge and the troopers were quickly overwhelmed and lynched, with broken bottles, sharpened sticks and bare hands.

The Mob surrounded the medical transport and attempted to break its way in, smashing the windows and pounding on the doors, which soon buckled and were then brutally forced open. Two of the medics were dragged, screaming, out of the van and torn apart by the very people they were trying to save. I saw a white coat, deeply stained with red, tossed victoriously into the air as The Mob howled in guttural triumph. Looking briefly away, I thought of my own abandoned jacket, in the alley, and shook my head in revulsion as the memory of what I had just done came flooding back.

The chief medic had somehow managed to clamber onto the roof of the van, out of the broken windscreen, and so delay his doom by a few futile moments. He stood, looking down at his attackers in terror and shouting in dishevelled panic, his mask long-since discarded. Perhaps he was pleading for his life or maybe he was praying to whatever god he professed faith in. I could not tell. Ultimately, it did not matter one iota.

The Mob began to work in symbiotic unison, rocking the vehicle back and forth as the medic clung on in desperation. It soon managed to tip the van over, crushing many of its own number in the process but ignoring their screams as the victim was delivered to the waiting fists and feet of the baying beast. The hapless doctor managed one quick scream, which was abruptly cut off, before he, too, was swallowed up by the ravenous, insatiable maw.

Now that it had tasted blood and there was no more prey, The Mob turned on itself to feed its mindless frenzy. I heard women scream as their bodies were seized and violated by lust-crazed males, I heard bones cracking as people were trampled underfoot, either caught in the melee or stamped wilfully to death, and I heard visceral cries of rage, aggression and pleasure spewing from mouths that would have, until a scant few weeks ago, spoken to each other in much more civilised tones.

Mercifully, as the throng boiled and seethed in The Mob's implosion, I heard approaching sirens and a police transport arrived on the scene, from the opposite direction to where I was standing. The officers jumped out, but there were only three: why always so few? Without any attempt at warnings or crowd control, they began firing their automatic weapons indiscriminately into the flock.

Corpses fell quickly and efficiently, in waves of blood and body matter, as the police firearms reaped their deadly harvest. A few rioters attempted to charge the officers, but they were swiftly cut down, with their battle cries still building in their throats. As the remnants of The Mob finally realised how desperate their situation had become, they broke and ran for their lives, with the gunmen picking off a few stragglers, for good measure, to make sure that they continued to flee.

When all that remained was a pile of twitching corpses, the police jumped into their vehicle and sped off, with sirens still blaring, no doubt to another similar scene elsewhere in the city: another state-sanctioned massacre. If only they were more numerous. Then, there would be a chance at restoring law and order, even if it had to be done so brutally. Pushing these thoughts aside with a conscious effort, I seized the opportunity to try and ascertain my friend's fate. I had to know for sure what had happened.

Her building was no longer visible. In fact, I was not even sure where it had been, as numerous scorched shadows were all that marked the street where tower blocks had once stood. I crossed the blood-soaked road gingerly and stood, for a moment, at the spot which I thought had been the entrance to her building. I could see no trace of anything human, no trace of anything at all, in fact.

She was gone, of that I was now sure. I was equally sure that I needed to get out of the city extremely quickly. Things were clearly worse than I had thought and would only get more and more desperate as the hours and days wore on.

As I began to pick my way back across the bodies that lay strewn across the tarmac, a few stirred and groaned, not yet dead but surely dying. Aware of the need for caution, I pressed my mask tightly over my face and shielded my eyes with my other hand. The air was full of moist droplets of bodily origin and that meant that the virus was present, too.

As I walked, a hand clasped feebly at my ankle and I looked down into the dimming eyes of a man at my feet, his other hand clutched ineffectually at the numerous ragged holes that dotted his torso. He looked incredibly frail and human as, drenched in his own and others' blood, he silently entreated me to help.

I felt nothing but a worrying sense of detachment as I stood and gazed impassively down at him dying. There was nothing I could, or wanted to, do for him. I could not spare any water to ease his passing, nor could I forget his recent actions as a member of the mob, which had displayed so little mercy or humanity to its victims. Now, he was begging me to show him a little compassion but, to my shame and surprise, I could muster none. I suppose that only by suffering ourselves can we truly empathise with the pain that we have inflicted on others. I had done, and seen, so much that morning that I could already feel my previously clear-cut sense of morals beginning to shift, beginning to harden. I was genuinely shocked by how quickly it seemed to be happening.

I turned away, preoccupied in thought, as the man at my feet became just another corpse with a bubbling, rattling sigh. I had to accept that my lady friend was obviously dead and now I had to look to my own defence. It was clear that I needed to get out of the city, and away from the madness engulfing it, immediately. I decided that catching a train was my only decent option, so I set off in the direction of the main station, with the slim hope that there would still be some services running on which to escape.

***

I suspected that things were seriously amiss from almost a kilometre away. I had been assailed by sirens, gunfire and screams echoing in the distance for almost all of my shadow-hugging journey thus far, but this was different. I could tell by the din and the way that the air hung, heavy and thick, that there were a lot of people in the station plaza, certainly more than I had ever previously known in the vicinity.

I could not hear any sounds that indicated violence but, after the events of that morning, I knew that I couldn't take any chances. With caution as a byword, I decided to have a look before I entered the square; it would definitely not be wise to merely amble up blindly. My experiences earlier on had taught me a new wariness and I felt more than a little nervous fear as I drew nearer.

There were a number of tall residential buildings overlooking the plaza but far enough away to make going into the square itself unnecessary, so I decided to climb to the top of one. That way, I'd be able to scout ahead of me and know what danger to expect before venturing towards the station.

Though a few side streets had been mostly demolished, with debris blocking my way, and a couple more were cordoned off, blocking access to them, I saw one leading to a large building, which was still relatively intact, and approached cautiously. To my relief, the road was also a dead end, so there was no danger of anyone approaching from the direction of the square and attacking me.

I cautiously entered the foyer, which was thankfully deserted, and stabbed at the button to call the lift, using the hem of my t-shirt as a makeshift glove to lessen any chance of picking up infection. I was not at all surprised when it failed to either move or open its doors; power interruptions had been growing more frequent over the last few weeks as what little electricity could still be produced was saved for essential uses only. Obviously, this elevator did not fall under the definition of 'essential', so I was forced to use my legs.

As I opened the door to the stairs, a blast of fetid air hit me full in the face and, despite my face covering, I gagged and instinctively brought up a hand to cover my mouth and nose. I hesitated, then stepped out into the stairwell and immediately saw the reason for the ungodly stench: faeces and rubbish lined the walls and covered the steps completely. The sheer volume, plus the relentless heat, had combined to accelerate their decomposition, that much was evident.

Clearly, the sewage system had broken down there much longer ago than in my area of town, where it was still working even that morning. Still, surely there was no need, nor excuse, for fouling one's own living space. If the sanitation system itself was down, who did the residents think would clean up their waste? In such times, it was important to do what one could to *lessen* the risk of transmitting the virus, but the inhabitants of this building seemed not to have got that memo.

I picked my way carefully through the filth as I set my sights on an open window, promising sweet relief, on the next landing. Reaching it, I leant my head gratefully out, pushed my mask to one side and took deep lungfuls of deliciously fresh air, before I steeled myself against the invasive stink and carried on up the stairs. The surrounding buildings blocked most of the natural light that would otherwise be coming into the stairwell and also, therefore, the view of the station square, at least from the few windows I could see, so I decided that the roof would be the best place to head for, even if it meant trudging another fifteen floors up.

Mercifully, the stench gradually diminished as I climbed higher, and my eyes finally stopped watering. Perhaps the inhabitants higher up the building were more civilised, or maybe they couldn't even be bothered to walk downstairs and, instead, just threw their excrement out of their windows, into the street below.

As I was passing the twelfth floor: the numbers written in huge lettering on the slightly ajar access door, I heard a woman sobbing on the landing within. I thought of how I had been unable to save my friend earlier and my heart fluttered at the possibility that I might be able to, at least, help *someone* a little that grim day. Using the hem of my t-shirt again rather than my bare hand, I cautiously pushed open the door leading to the apartments on that floor and I immediately gagged, as the all-too-familiar aroma of rotting rubbish and human waste instantly powered out to greet me, in a potent, full-frontal, nasal assault.

The place was deathly quiet, apart from the sound of the woman weeping, which seemed to be coming from further down the hallway. I moved silently down the landing, tiptoeing carefully through the filth and refuse lining the floor, towards the noise. It seemed that most of the apartments were empty, their doors open: some hanging off their hinges as if kicked in, but then I saw her, sitting alone in an open doorway with her head buried in her hands.

I moved closer, concern welling in my soul but, just as I was about to call out to the woman, I realised that her hands were covered in blood and the words died in my throat as I stopped, suddenly motionless. I tried to back away silently, fear suddenly running cold and thick through my veins, but she must have sensed my presence and looked up at me with a gaze that converted my fear into a debilitating terror, as complete as I had not imagined possible.

I turned and fled headlong back into the cloying stairwell, no longer noticing the stink, and slammed the fire door firmly shut behind me. I searched vainly for something to block the entrance but, finding nothing immediately in reach, turned and mounted the remaining stairs in what would, surely, have been a world record time, if anyone were still measuring such things.

Upon reaching the gangway that gave access to the roof, through a small service hatch, I climbed up it as quickly as I could and slammed the tiny opening firmly shut behind me. I contemplated kicking away the ladder but knew that would only strand me up there and would not stop any determined pursuer.

I looked fervently around and spied a heavy concrete block among a nearby pile of rubble. I grabbed it and strained and heaved, using every ounce of strength in my aching sinews, until I managed to roll it on top of the service hatch. That would surely be enough to deter anyone who might be following and would provide a permanent barrier to anyone else wishing to climb up. What was more, it would enable me to stay as long as I wished on the roof and, more importantly, to stay there undisturbed. I was quickly realising that the biggest threat to me now was no longer the virus but was actually other people.

The roof was wide and relatively flat, one of those largely homogenous modern buildings that could be found in any city, anywhere in the world. In the middle was a small hut, probably a service office, that looked promising as a temporary shelter. I immediately sensed that I would be safe there, for more or less the first time since leaving home, and I was tempted to linger a while on that feeling but more immediately, I needed to assess the situation in the station plaza below.

The din was, once more, deafeningly loud now that I was outside again, though quieter and more distant than it had been at street level. I approached the lip of the building's roof that overlooked the train terminus, with the hut behind me, and settled down on my haunches, minimising my silhouette as I looked out over the square, which was teeming with untold hordes of people.

Peering down into the plaza, my surgically enhanced eyes auto-focused instantly, despite the considerable distance, and enabled me to see what was happening as clearly as if I were much, much closer. I silently thanked fate for the inspired foresight to have had the surgery while the world was still civilised. The operation suddenly seemed like a very wise investment and the financial inconvenience of its considerable expense was rapidly fading into an anachronism.

The square below was packed with humanity, from all walks of life. They were doing nothing but standing, watching the station itself and shouting incoherently, yet they seemed to be growing angrier and angrier with each passing minute. There appeared to be little attempt by anyone in the crowd to take precautions against the spread of the virus. Indeed, quite a few even had banners proclaiming that the whole pandemic was a lie: a conspiracy. I was extremely glad that I was a safe distance away.

The entrance to the station building was clear of civilians but heavily guarded by both soldiers and armed military police in protective suits. It was not immediately apparent what the source of the crowd's ire might be, so I, too, just sat still and watched. It certainly did not seem very likely that I would be getting a train out of there after all, so I was in no rush whatsoever and decided to rest a moment while waiting to see what developments occurred.

I saw a sudden movement and a transport emerged steadily from the station, gaining speed on its magnetic rails as it pulled out of its berth, presumably en route to leaving the city. I had no way of knowing who the passengers were but, judging by the guards, barriers and the rancour of the people in the square, the great unwashed, myself included, were not in possession of tickets.

As the crowd watched the train leave to presumed safety, large sections of it began to howl and churn in indignation and fury. Stones, bottles: anything to hand was thrown at the carriages but the machine ploughed on imperviously, with nothing but a few cracked windows to show for all the massed rage being directed at it. The guards attempted to control the situation by firing warning shots over the heads of the more prominent troublemakers, while loudspeakers assailed the masses, barking instructions, though I could not really hear what was being said, due to the din and the distance from my elevated sanctuary.

The soldiers succeeded in pushing back the throngs of people, away from the station entrance, and appeared to placate them a little but only just. Then suddenly, from the west side of the plaza, a convoy of slick, black vehicles appeared, driving silently at high speed along the narrow corridor that the sentries were, just about, maintaining between the tracks and the crowd. As the cars screeched to a stop outside the grand staircase that provided access to the terminal, more soldiers emerged from inside the building to bring aid to the passengers alighting from the vehicles.

It was immediately clear that these new arrivals, dressed expensively in jewelled masks, suits and designer dresses, had places reserved on the next train out and I realised that this was an evacuation of the city's elite.

Evidently, escape *was* possible for those who had the money and/or connections to book a ticket out of there, leaving the rest of their species to their doom in that festering pit of humanity, without a second thought. When the die of survival was cast, it was everyone for themselves and wealth, position and power were what made you one of the key players. I had none of those. All I had was a semi-decent brain and that would have to be enough.

As the new arrivals were being quickly marched into the station by the soldiers, the crowd resumed its churning and jeering but this time much more vociferously, stoked by righteous indignation at the injustice playing out before their eyes. It was now undeniable, now crystal-clear what was happening and the people thronging the square, the forsaken masses, did not like it one bit. They began to surge forward against the barriers, with much greater violence and intent than before, and the sheer weight of their numbers quickly began to show a result.

The barricades started to first bend, then break as hordes upon hordes of screaming souls clambered over them in their blind desperation to escape, or perhaps in a savage lust for vengeance and blood.

The first people to hit the hallowed ground beyond the barriers were cut down, brutally, by the weapons of the security forces, but there were too many for them to stop, far too many. The second wave of rioters hurdled the bodies of their erstwhile comrades on the floor and charged, en masse, towards the entrance.

The soldiers who did not immediately throw down their arms and run were trampled where they stood, their bullets useless against the sheer weight of howling humanity that engulfed and quickly destroyed them. A previously unseen squad of troops attempted to stem the tide, emerging from within the station with their guns firing, but they, too, dropped their weapons and fled in blind panic as The Mob reached the ornate steps, rushing up them like a living, baying tsunami, intent on murder.

The train started to pull out of the station, with the last passengers rushing to get on and close the doors behind them, but it was moving slowly, much too slowly, to make good its escape. Barriers were falling the length of the square and a huge, roiling torrent of bodies stormed the locomotive from the side in a solid, organic mass. A few hapless souls spilled onto the tracks and stood in the machine's way, defiantly howling as they were first effortlessly crushed under its weight and then torn apart by its magnetic fields.

Whether their self-sacrifice was intentional or not, their corpses had the effect of slowing the engine down and, at that same moment, a fresh wave of people rushed the vehicle from behind, along the tracks, coming from within the station building itself, which had obviously been completely overrun. They easily caught up with the train, bogged down in the quagmire of human remains it had just created. The Mob swarmed onto the roofs, breaking windows and forcing open the carriage doors in its desperation to catch a ride out of the city. I saw people being thrown, screaming, out of the exits and windows and their helpless bodies trampled underfoot in the mad scramble to get aboard.

Then, the train abruptly stopped advancing and began to slide, slowly, sideways. Somewhere in the station, whether wilfully or incidentally, the power had been cut. The magnetic traction of the rails no longer held the carriages in place, and they immediately began to feel the effects of gravity pull on them. The air cushions, however, still provided lift, keeping the vehicle off the floor and ensuring that it kept on moving. The cars began to slip smoothly and inexorably down the small embankment that elevated the tracks from the square.

People panicked and tried desperately to move out of the way as the train picked up speed and slewed towards them, but they were too slow and too densely packed to successfully flee. The runaway carriages cut a huge and bloody swathe through those unfortunate enough to be in their way as they careered wildly. Eventually, the train slowed to a halt, its air cushions clogging with the ground-up bodies of the casualties it had created and ceasing to function as a result.

Upon seeing the carnage, a large section of the crowd broke away and fled the square, screaming in blind panic, but the overwhelming majority did not, and The Mob renewed its howling as it stormed the now-stationary train, from all angles.

I watched in silent horror as flailing figure after flailing figure was dragged out and tossed, shrieking in terror, onto the ground, to be torn apart by the very people they were supposed, in society's pyramid of power, to control. There was no moral victory for the masses, however, it was just senseless carnage and though I was no longer surprised at the scenes below, I was still disgusted at what I was seeing and that was, to me at least, somewhat reassuring.

The indignation, the frustration of those left behind and the storming of the train, either in an attempt to escape or as a form of protest, that I could understand. However, what was happening in the square was something else, something completely different. It was murder, simple and brutal, and nothing could ever justify that. There were no possible excuses for what I was seeing.

It was not killing in self-defence; it was merely mindless slaughter. It seemed to me that nothing could warrant crossing the line between the two and yet I was horrified, again, at how easily that sacrosanct boundary was being breeched below me in the station square. A few solitary gunshots echoed from within the station building but they were quickly silenced. The Mob had control of the area.

I wondered briefly, *what had become of the other train?* I thought, hopefully, that there was a fair chance it had made it out of the city, but I suppose I knew the truth, deep down. The loss of power would have also derailed the earlier departure. Perhaps it had derailed others, too: I had no idea how many had already left before I arrived.

In all probability, the scene I was now watching was being played out all across the country, perhaps even across the whole planet. From what I was seeing of our true human nature, and especially that day, I could envisage blood running thick on the streets of cities worldwide. I wondered, too, whether the soldiers and police, who had died attempting to defend their paymasters, had possessed train tickets. If not, as was probably the case, why would they have so readily given up their lives? Did they believe in something, believe in a cause, and die for that ideal or were they just too conditioned to see things as they really were and choose the right side?

Wearily, I turned away as The Mob rampaged triumphantly across the plaza, breaking up into smaller pockets as its ardour dissipated. The day was theirs and their enemy dead, so it would surely not be long before they turned on one another and I did not feel the need to witness any more bloodshed.

My plan to take a train was now as obsolete as human decency and compassion and the streets were, evidently, becoming more and more dangerous with each passing hour. I was suddenly faced with a distinct lack of options, so I decided on staying where I was, at least until nightfall. I hurriedly checked the stone over the hatch and, to my relief, it hadn't budged. No one had even tried to come up and the rooftop was probably the safest place I could be for the moment.

With a sudden spasm, I realised that I had a more pressing concern, although it was a purely natural one: I desperately needed the toilet. In the chaos of the morning's events, I had not realised that I needed to go but now I really had no choice in the matter. Things were, all of a sudden, urgent.

To my shame, I thought first of the building's stairwell but immediately recoiled in disgust, both at the idea and at myself. It was not a feasible option. I was not yet ready to stoop to that level, neither literally nor figuratively. My apartment had, until that morning, continued to have both running water and sewage disposal and I was not prepared to relinquish that one mundane aspect of civilised behaviour that had remained constant in my life, despite the regression all around.

My state of revulsion seemed laughably trivial when one considered all that I had done and seen already but I was determined to find another way, a way that allowed me to retain some modicum of human dignity in the face of all this senseless violence and savagery.

I walked across the roof to the small structure in its centre, thinking that there may be a toilet inside that I could use, even if it would probably no longer flush. Trying the handle, the door was locked and, when I looked inside, the building seemed unoccupied. Recoiling in sudden alarm, I cursed myself sharply for omitting to check whether it was inhabited or not when I had first arrived on the roof. I then remembered that I was very new to this kind of animal-instinct survival. As such, I quickly contented myself with feeling lucky and chalked it up to experience.

I needed to gain entry, so I lifted a small piece of concrete block from the floor and bashed my way through a panel in the door, breaking the glass and unlocking it from the inside before stepping through as it opened. It really was as easy as it looked in the films.

For a brief second, I thought of the things I'd done recently and how I had never been anything but a law-abiding citizen, all my life, until a few short hours ago. Now, I had no second thoughts about breaking into a locked room, into private property, and even the dried blood on my clothes from earlier that morning was becoming merely literal and no longer metaphorical.

I could clearly appreciate that the world I had once known was changing irrevocably, eroding rapidly, and a little breaking and entering was extremely small peanuts compared to what else I'd got up to. I was already au fait with the bigger, brutal picture and busy reconciling myself mentally, and disturbingly quickly, with what my survival might necessitate me doing.

I looked around me in mild surprise; the room was larger than it appeared from the outside. It looked like it had been used as an office for the building's security guard or caretaker, until fairly recently. I checked that my face mask was still securely in place, just in case, then searched in vain for a toilet but, to my consternation, there was nowhere to relieve myself. A small fridge in the corner caught my eye and I cracked it open, more out of habit than hunger, but one whiff of its rotting contents was enough to make me slam it immediately shut again, recoiling in horror and gagging.

My abdomen was starting to ache and churn aggressively, as nature grew more and more insistent and I really could not hold back any longer. I hurriedly grabbed an unused roll of kitchen paper that had been left, mercifully, in a small sink area and rushed outside to relieve myself behind the shack. I swallowed my pride and crouched on the ground as an animal, or our archaic ancestors, would have done.

As I squatted there, I felt more than faintly ashamed. It was strange that I seemed to feel much more regret at that one trivial thing than almost anything else, excluding that morning's killing, since my cosy little existence had so abruptly changed. A little part of me already wondered if, in the long-term, I would succeed in keeping my civilised perspective on life, and my sanity.

Wearily, I used the kitchen roll, then climbed to my feet and pulled my trousers up again, wondering where and when

I'd be able to wash my hands properly. For now, I sparingly cleaned them with a little sanitiser from my bag. As I washed, I could still hear screams and cries coming from the square, but they seemed to have somewhat diminished in magnitude and merely provided a soundtrack to my despair; a background of ambient white noise that was no longer shocking nor even significant.

I had evidently reached a new low, as the fight-or-flight instinct began to subside, and I was starting to realise that I was losing something, losing a little part of me. Worryingly, there seemed to be no way that I would ever be able to regain it. I had already seen and done too much for me to be able to segue smoothly back to the life I once had.

As it was, nothing much separated me from the savages in the square below. They, too, had relinquished whatever it was that we could, once upon a time, have claimed distinguished us from the other animals on this planet. I could not shake the feeling that the changes being wrought, in all of us and society itself, were irrevocable. We had regressed too far, too quickly for us to ever, it seemed, have a chance of going back to what we knew as normality a few short weeks ago.

I walked a few steps but then squatted on my haunches, once again, and covered my face with my hands as a crushing epiphany hit me: I did not have a clue how to proceed.

As the adrenaline began to fully wear off, I also realised that I was hungry and extremely tired. The dull pounding in my head told me that I was also quite dehydrated. In addition, I was, by default, trapped up there on the roof.

However dangerous the streets had been earlier on, I now knew them to have become ten times worse, in a few short hours. I was, for the time being, besieged by the chaos still swelling in and around the station square and the risk of attack from the denizens of the building below me if I ventured down again. Despite that, I was not in any immediate danger, or so it seemed, and I felt I could afford to relax a little, for the first time in hours, and tend to other, physical needs.

Reaching for my bag, I noticed that it was slightly open. I looked inside and cursed: the food and water that I had packed were nowhere to be found. The provisions had either fallen out during my earlier flight or, more probably, been stolen whilst I was distracted watching the destruction of my friend's building. I would have to find a meal elsewhere.

I turned back and re-entered the rooftop lodge, my parched throat and growling stomach leading me to cautiously loosen the door of the fridge once more. I was forced to put my arm over my mask-covered mouth and nose as I did so, to try and block the odour that, even with the door only slightly ajar, was already seeping out in noxious tendrils to test both my resolve and hunger. Even worse, I knew from my previous whiff of the contents that nothing remotely appetising could possibly await me within. However, I was starting to feel a little desperate, as my head throbbed insistently, and there were certainly no other options for sustenance in the immediate vicinity. I took a deep breath and braved a look inside.

Contrary to what the overpowering, cloying stench of decay might have led one to believe, there was not much at all on offer inside the fridge. On the top shelf were the remains of what must have been fruit, of some kind, but it was now unrecognisable, shrivelled and black from the heat and humidity. It was of no use to me at all. Underneath was some *seriously* mature cheese and a packet of utterly putrid meat, so rotten it was almost liquid, although mercifully still in its cellophane packaging. Obviously, I had found the source of the unbelievable stink.

"Well, at least the bacteria are thriving," I whispered to myself and smiled stupidly, amused at my own rubbish joke and definitely starting to unwind little by little with each passing minute, despite my precarious predicament.

I briefly toyed with the idea of throwing away the rancid meat, maybe even hurling it over the side of the building and into the square below. I chuckled to myself as I imagined it hitting a rabid rioter full in their unsuspecting face. After careful reflection, I decided not to, despite the potential for comedic satisfaction, as I could not risk drawing attention to myself with reckless actions and, more importantly, I did not want to put my hand anywhere near that festering mess. Instead, I pulled the cheese gingerly out and slammed the door tightly shut, sealing in both the smell and all that rotten matter.

I hurriedly made my way outside and took deep lungfuls of untainted air, leaving the shack door wide open for the residual smell to dissipate. Having second thoughts, I ran back inside and opened all the windows I could find, to get a fresh breeze flowing through, before making my way once more out onto the roof. As well as dissipating the stench, the draught would also clear out any residual viral particles in the room's atmosphere, if the scientists were to be believed.

I sat in the warm, afternoon sun and studied my prize. It was a large block of processed cheese, still tightly wrapped in plastic but mouldy nonetheless due to the fetid heat sealed inside the refrigerator unit. Still, it did not look too bad underneath the top layer, so I ripped the packaging off then, forgetting about the knife in my waistband, pulled and scraped the fur off the top as best I could with no tools, just using my bare hands. I turned it over a few times, eyeing the remaining white flecks with suspicion, before wolfing it down, holding my breath as I did so to lessen the impact of the flavour as much as possible.

It was not the best meal I had ever eaten, far from it, but it was immeasurably better than nothing and it didn't even taste that bad, certainly nowhere near as foul as I had expected. I slowed down a little and savoured the last mouthful. It was mature enough to make my eyes water, but it was still recognisably cheese, and would, quite possibly, even have been classed as a delicacy in certain parts of the world.

No sooner had I swallowed the last piece, however, than my thirst came raging back and I decided to brave the kitchen inside, again, to look for some water. I stepped warily through the door, nostrils twitching in anticipation of attack, but was relieved to discover that the smell had largely gone and there was a cool, refreshing breeze wafting through the room.

I walked in and headed straight for the small sink in the corner. I did not bother to even try the taps as I knew they would be dry. Instant access to drinkable water was something which we had, a few weeks before, all taken for granted. Now, it already seemed an unimaginable luxury.

Opening the cupboard door beneath hopefully, I found a large bottle of what was, according to the label at least, mineral water. The seal on the cap was broken: it had obviously been opened, but it looked and smelled fine. At any rate, the thirst that was assailing my throat was becoming increasingly insistent and my headache seemed to be pumping a deep tiredness all through my body. I knew that debilitating dehydration was not too far away, so I took a chance and drained the bottle gratefully in one long, measured swig. I then sat down on the floor, sighing contentedly.

I gazed smugly around my rooftop sanctuary and broke into a wide smile of self-satisfied triumph. Despite my situation, stuck on the roof and stranded by the waves of violence breaking on the city below, my belly was comfortably full, and I swore that I could already feel my headache receding, though that was probably more likely to be psychological than real. Nevertheless, it was a welcome sensation when compared to everything I had experienced so far that day. Even if it proved to be only a temporary respite, then I was still determined to enjoy the moment.

Inside my shelter, the noise from outside, the noise of my world, my city imploding and devouring itself was almost inaudible and I felt very secure and cocooned up there. I felt even more so when I slammed the door shut, locking it firmly from within.

I closed the windows until they were only slightly ajar, in order to let in a little air, deciding at the same time to stay there for a while, or at least until I had come up with a viable plan of escape from the city. I needed a new course of action, one which would, hopefully, make my long-term survival far more likely and my rooftop hideaway would be a great place to think of one. I sat down, leaning back against the wall and dozed off almost immediately.

***

I awoke with a start, instantly alert, and looked thoughtfully out of the main window. Judging by the sun's position in the sky, it was late afternoon, that heavy stillness just as the day begins to segue into early evening. The temperature had dropped somewhat, but it was still very warm.

I decided it would be best to spend the night there. If I retired now, I could get a long, restorative sleep in yet still rise at first light, again, and set off before most people were awake. Perhaps I could 'source' a bicycle, or even a powered vehicle, and get out of the city before its murderous denizens stirred once more and resumed their newfound savagery. The world might well be ending, with opportunistic scavengers profiting from its death throes, but even hyenas needed to sleep. It was not much of a plan, to be honest, but it was the best I could come up with, at least for the moment.

I yawned slowly as a sudden exhaustion swept through my body. I looked around. There was no bed in the room, but I quickly found an old curtain rolled up in the corner and lay down on the hard floor with it over me, using my backpack as a rather lumpy pillow. It was not perfect, but I would have to make do and at least it was not cold. As it was, I was so tired that my thoughts began to drift into abstraction almost immediately and I was just closing my eyes when I sat up with a start. The brutal reality of my situation suddenly slammed back to the forefront of my mind and with it came the same, debilitating fear that was becoming a familiar companion.

I climbed gingerly to my feet, my limbs screaming in protest at the rest so suddenly denied them, and propped a folded chair under and against the door handle, jamming it firmly closed. It would not keep a determined intruder out indefinitely, but it would at least give me some warning as I slept and, hopefully, allow me a slim chance of getting away.

I dragged my 'bed' next to a small rear window that could prove a means of escape, if necessary, then I closed my eyes and surrendered to the deep waves of fatigue that were rolling and breaking throughout my entire body, dragging me down into the blissful oblivion of slumber.

***

I jerked violently into a sitting position, my body covered in a light sheen of perspiration and shaking in the cooler air. Something had subtly changed in my environment and had caused me to stir: instantly awake and alert to danger.

I sat, perfectly still, and listened but I could hear nothing at all, nor could my sleep-muddled brain discern what, if anything, was different. I had no idea what the time was, but it was almost completely dark outside, so I must have slept for four or maybe five hours.

Over the last few weeks, the lights that had once illuminated the whole city had gradually shut off across the metropolis, district by district, street by street and had left us all at the mercy of a total darkness that we had once thought vanquished and controlled. As well as awakening deeper, primal instincts in my fellow humans, this had also made it very difficult to gauge the time once the sun had retired, a mundane yet irritating consequence of an absence of artificial light.

Though the night had not yet completed its inevitable conquest of the day, I could barely see my hand in front of my face. I readjusted my mask, rose to my feet and stood, teeth chattering, for a few seconds in the cool breeze, which ebbed across my moisture-soaked skin in relentless currents.

My clothes were damp and clung to my body like a sodden shroud, but I was loathe to change into my only spare set so soon. As my nostrils wrinkled in protest at the acrid, warm smell of my own sweat, I stamped and shivered in an attempt to stay warm, while listening out for signs that anything was amiss.

I first attempted to ascertain that I was not in any immediate danger. Cautiously, I peeked out of the windows and confirmed that I was still alone on the rooftop before I slipped my backpack on once more and headed outside to relieve myself, against the back wall of the poor hut, again. It was much easier the second time as I wistfully watched the rivulets of urine drift down the wall and slowly colonise the asphalt surface in micro-inundations. I wondered, briefly, how long it would take for me to consider that kind of behaviour normal. I also wondered when I would next find anything to drink, to replace the precious water that I was now losing from my system.

I shuddered when I considered that I may be forced to drink my own liquid waste in the very near future but then I thrust that thought from my mind with a determined shake of my head. Thankfully, we were not at that stage yet. I walked to the edge of the roof and glanced out over the station square, afraid of what I might see, but all seemed quiet, apart from a few scattered fires still burning meekly. I could see nothing else but the occasional shadowy figure passing in front of the flames.

It was deathly, unnaturally silent; perhaps that had woken me from my slumber. Like a hunting cat, I padded across the roof to the other side, which looked out over a central, paved courtyard. This small communal space was enclosed on all sides by four housing complexes, of which the rear walls of the building where I was sheltering formed one part. In happier times, it would have provided a place for leisure and relaxation, somewhere for the children living in the surrounding apartments to amuse themselves. That night, it held nothing but horror, as I was very soon to find out.

The courtyard had been deserted earlier on, the local residents no doubt joining in the 'festivities' in the station square, or perhaps lying dead somewhere. It was still unnervingly quiet but, as I cautiously peered over the lip of the roof, to my surprise the space was now full of people standing without moving, holding makeshift torches, whose flames flickered and danced eerily in the deepening darkness.

I stopped, frozen, not moving for fear of being noticed. Despite the large crowd, the entire area was preternaturally silent and the hairs rose suddenly, and violently, on the back of my neck, refusing to return to normal as I looked down.

I stood motionlessly and just watched, for about a minute. It was clear that the assembled people were waiting for something, or maybe for someone. Nobody moved nor spoke, not even a whisper. There were at least a hundred people gathered where, until very recently, children had played as residents whiled away lazy afternoons in the sunshine. Now, something altogether more sinister was undoubtedly playing itself out before my eyes, but I hadn't the faintest idea yet what that was.

My instincts screamed at me, told me to run far from that place, but a twisted curiosity, a horrified fascination transfixed me and forced me to remain where I was. I had to know what was happening, however disturbing, or it would forever haunt my idle thoughts, like an unsolved mystery or a set of permanently misplaced keys. In morbid fascination, I lowered myself slowly, silently, onto my stomach and crawled forward. I stopped where I could see clearly over the edge of the roof but would not myself be visible to those down below, should any restless or inquisitive eyes happen to gaze upwards towards my vantage point.

I glanced over the assembled throng, studying their faces, which were illuminated spectrally in the torchlight, and saw men, women and children: the old to the very young in the crowd. All ages and walks of life were represented. They were packed tightly together, with scant regard for recent public health advice. None that I could see were taking any precautions against the virus; were they immune or merely ignorant? There was a small group of men solemnly stoking a raging bonfire, which had been set underneath a diminutive, sorry-looking willow tree in the centre of the square. The trunk had been stripped of all its branches, apart from one thick bough that hung out over the small but intense blaze, with its leaves and shoots curling in the heat from below.

The men worked silently and determinedly, fanning the flames and feeding them, regularly, with bits of debris that they picked up from the floor; if there was one advantage of widespread destruction, then readily available fuel for fires would surely be it. All the assembled people, however, had their eyes trained on the building to the right of the one I was on. Not a single person was watching the fire, which was, to me at least, by far the most interesting thing in the vicinity.

I followed the gazes of the throng and saw that all their attention was fixed on the entrance, or the exit, to the complex. I wondered what on earth could be so captivating but a nagging, sick feeling in the pit of my stomach warned me that, perhaps, I would not want to know.

Suddenly, the sounds of a violent scuffle echoed from the foyer and the expectant crowd leaned forward in collective anticipation, beginning to sway and murmur softly as one, though the words were indistinct. In a flash of sudden action, a group of about ten people spilled out from the double doors and bustled into the square, jostling and shouting.

Once they had cleared the entrance way, a man, clearly in charge, swaggered out with an exaggerated flourish. The crowd, again as one, let out a gasp of collective admiration upon his appearance and he acknowledged his followers with a broad, wicked smile and a pompous wave. Then, he slowly, measuredly took his place at the top of the short set of ornate steps that led down into the square. His stage was set.

He stood, in full view of the assembled throng, and gestured grandly in the direction of his companions: a posse of burly men, who held a man and a woman, tightly restrained, in their grasp. Though they both struggled, the captives were no match for their laughing assailants, who lifted them, triumphantly, for all the crowd to see, before frog-marching them to the centre of the square, stopping just to the left of the bonfire.

At a signal from the leader: a quick chop with his left hand, they were both beaten to their knees, their heads held up to force their gaze on the main star of this disturbing horror show. The male hostage attempted to rise to his feet and spat, unsuccessfully, at his smiling tormentor but a vicious elbow from one of the henchmen knocked him heavily to the ground. He was immediately dragged back to his knees, with his head lolling dazedly and his mouth and nose bloody.

Once he was satisfied that the captives were securely restrained, the grinning instigator brushed himself down and then turned back to face his expectant crowd. Although more than a few necks strained and jostled discreetly to get a better view, not a single person had moved from their position in all the time since his arrival.

The black-clothed figure paused a few seconds, for theatrical effect, then gestured with another exaggerated flourish towards the hapless pair as he began a warped diatribe. My trepidation became genuine dread. I felt nauseous with the realisation of impending horror.

"Brothers, sisters, children of the present and defenders of the future. We are, all of us, assembled here because we are curators and protectors of the one noble truth. We alone have the intelligence, we alone have the presence of mind to see that this cursed pestilence is divine retribution, wrought upon us all, in penance for the sins of the wicked intruders who live among us.

"We gather here tonight, in this square, as an island of natural purity in a vast ocean of human filth. We gather here tonight to take a stand against the evil that has permeated this city, against the evil that has permeated this entire country. Arm in arm, strong in our unity and unwavering in our faith, we face the repercussions of a society that is corrupt, a society that is rotten and weak. It has fallen to us, the enlightened remnants in this dying metropolis, to defend ourselves against this plague, this *pestilence*, which threatens to consume everything we have worked for and all that we believe in."

He paused, with impeccable dramatic timing, and I could see heads in the crowd nodding their assent and murmuring their approval. Despite the dread in my heart at what might be about to happen, I could not help but shake my head, not for the first time, at the stupidity of the gathered masses for uncritically swallowing such a crock of half-baked, mock-heroic rubbish. There was sound, there was fury, for sure, but not a single word had any significance, nor any true value.

"We stand here with our children, with our loved ones, with our parents and with our friends. Look, now, into their eyes and you will see an innocent, untainted soul, undeserving of this cruel fate that has been prescribed for them. And so, we must begin our divine mission by cleansing *ourselves*, cleansing *tonight*, cleansing on our own doorstep. We must begin by purging and purifying the very roots of this plague and we will do it *here* and we will do it *now*.

"We have lived too long amongst these plague-carriers, trusting them, helping them, befriending them, for all our lives, up until this very moment. Yet, we knew not the error of our ways. We were not aware of the latent danger in our midst until it was almost too late.

"Now, we are aware. Now, we have seen the one noble truth, *our* truth, and that unswerving certitude dictates that all traitors *MUST* be purified in the cleansing flames of absolution. It must be done so that through their suffering, we, too, shall be saved. For only by our actions shall we distinguish ourselves from the unclean, from the infected, and prepare ourselves for the salvation that awaits us; the salvation we truly *deserve*."

The crowd roared in visceral approval as the demagogue reached his rabid, spittle-flecked crescendo. Things did not bode at all well for the two captives and I felt the ever-growing knot of nausea twisting alarmingly in my stomach at the thought of what was to come.

How could people so blindly believe such insanity? The truth was that most who remained untouched by the virus were, by now, very possibly immune, especially those who lived in the large towns and cities, and those who were already carrying it were dead men (or women) walking; they could not be saved. The contagion had already ravaged its way through the population with hideous speed and not even the finest minds in the land, with all the resources of a wealthy government, could do anything to slow or even contain its spread.

Even less could be done about the madness and base stupidity that had propagated, much more virulently, in the virus's wake. The hapless couple in the square tonight were seemingly about to become another two casualties of a deranged, cognitive paralysis, which appeared to have taken a firm hold of most of humanity. They were in the hands of an obvious lunatic, and the only thing worse than a lunatic with illusions of grandeur was a religious lunatic, with delusions of divine grandeur. Clearly, things were not going to end well.

As the crowd nodded their agreement, with a few even cheering, the demagogue turned with an exaggerated flourish to gesture at the captives. He flashed a wide, wicked smile, his teeth glinting like flickering daggers in the bright firelight as he played and relished the moment. Even at a distance, although it was dark, my augmented eyesight saw the tell-tale signs of infection: red flecks on his teeth and blood-filled spittle gathering in the corners of his lips. He wiped his mouth quickly with his sleeve and the traces were suddenly gone, but the contagion remained, coursing through his body and dooming him as surely as a gangrenous wound. He did not have long to live.

Perhaps his condition could explain his insanity, could possibly explain his fervour but it certainly could not excuse it. In desperation and fear at facing certain death, he was perverting the susceptible minds of the ignorant masses with violent, destructive fantasies. The human desire to survive was so strong that it could be twisted, providing enough justification for the man beneath me to relegate others to the status of mere pawns, objects to be used for his own selfish gain, regardless of whether that gain was imagined or real. Who knew whether or not he genuinely believed the bile he was producing but he was, no doubt, desperate enough to give anything a try, even at the expense of innocent lives.

Of course, it was a dilemma that we all had to face, and the ramifications were not at all lost on me. I had already killed someone, in order to survive, but deeming it to have been necessary did not negate either the literal or metaphorical blood on my hands. Although I had already done much that shocked me, what line would I, personally, have to cross in order to become that man below? More pertinently, how close was I, already, to crossing it?

My reverie was abruptly halted as the figure began to speak again, his eyes closed and arms wide open in a sick parody of a messianic pose.

"By the power that is vested in me and through me speaks, I now pronounce judgement upon these two heretics," he boomed. The crowd was hushed in awe and eager expectation. The fanatic turned to the male captive and jabbed an accusatory finger, bony and long, at him.

"You came, unbidden, uninvited, to this land and we welcomed you with open arms and hearts. In return, you brought with you the seeds of your foreign illness and *pestilence*. You repaid our kindness with death and our tolerance with disease. You must pay for these sins with *your* life; you must die to halt the spread. Let this be a *MESSAGE* to all your kind."

The crowd roared into life, baying suddenly for blood as if all that silence had been unbearable. With a quick gesture to his henchmen, the demagogue retired a few feet away and looked skywards in a ghastly appropriation of saintliness as the horror truly began.

The male captive was brought struggling to his feet and his hands bound. He attempted to kick and bite at his captors as they cruelly held his arms behind his back, but he was quickly subdued. The female captive cried out to him, but her words were indistinct, and she was swiftly thumped on the back of the head to silence her.

The man managed to turn to his partner and whisper something, inaudible at distance, before he was viciously pushed into the waiting throng of spectators. They instantly became a mass of seething bodies as every man, woman and child sought to lay a hand, or foot, upon the unfortunate victim to punch, claw, gouge, kick or stamp. A few segments of The Mob went down, too, bowled over by the weight of their fellows pressing in on them in their eagerness for blood.

Although they were caught in their comrades' viciousness, becoming collateral, biological damage, nobody stopped to help. The others were blinded by their bloodlust and tore apart even their erstwhile brethren with glee in the confusion. It was over very quickly and, mercifully, the screams did not last for very long.

At a signal from the leader, one of his men brandished a flare gun, fired in the air and shouted something: one word. The Mob retreated almost instantly to its waiting position, resuming the previous eerie silence and swaying. The hackles on the back of my neck rose at the sight. There was nothing remotely natural about what I was witnessing.

Now that the attackers had withdrawn, I could see torn, trampled bodies lying on the ground and, in the flickering torchlight, dark pools of what must have been blood slowly spreading and staining the paving stones.

I counted three corpses in all: the male captive plus two unfortunates, torn apart where they had fallen. No words were necessary as the henchmen picked up the man's corpse and threw it, unceremoniously, on the fire. Once done, the stooges looked to their leader for guidance and he nodded, solemnly. The lackeys then dragged the two remaining bodies: one female, one a male child, and dumped them, too, into the blaze.

As the flames roared and danced, relishing this new fuel, the false prophet lowered his head. It was a grotesque pastiche of respect, in light of what had just happened, but the crowd took it as sincere and followed suit. A faint waft of cooking meat reached me up on the roof, permeating through my mask, and I gagged, lifting my t-shirt to cover my mouth and nose. Though my garment was caked in dried blood and filth and did not smell in any way pleasant itself, it was infinitely preferable to the stench of human flesh being barbecued, like supermarket sausages in a summer garden.

As the bodies burned, I turned my gaze to the female captive. The tears of pain and humiliation had dried on her face, which was smeared with blood from the blows of her attackers, but her back was straight and proud as she stared, stoically, at the fire. She had clearly gone through the initial, debilitating fear and was resigned to facing her fate with dignity.

My shock at what I was seeing had begun to wear off somewhat, too, and I turned to thinking of what, if anything, I could do to try and save the poor soul below as she knelt there, calmly awaiting a no-doubt horrific death. I had no weapons that could help. A gun would have been perfect, but I did not have one and I had no chance of overpowering so many people with nothing but my knife.

A superhero of old could definitely have rescued her but, sadly, they were very much fictitious and even their authors were probably dead, dying or otherwise deranged by now. I had to do something, nevertheless. I couldn't just sit there and watch another innocent be casually butchered by those psychopaths.

Perhaps, if I could cause some kind of a distraction, I might be able to help. I could not achieve anything from where I was, though. I was exposed and cornered and anything I did would likely draw immediate attention to my presence and, inevitably, lead to my rapid appearance as extra, impromptu fodder for the raging flames. I needed to get down to street level before I attempted anything. That would also give me time to think of some kind of plan.

As I started back towards the ladder that led down, I heard the demagogue begin again and I peeked once more over the edge to listen.

"As for *you*," he pointed another accusing finger at the woman, hastily wiping flecks of red drool from his mouth as his tension increased. "One of our own who chose to lie with a foreign devil, who chose to betray her people and compatriots with the affection and respect she showed to an unclean...*barbarian*. You gave him a reason to stay, you facilitated his existence among us and you even bore him *children*.

"The offspring are young, it is not too late for them to be correctly raised but *you*, you are a traitor of the worst kind, deserving of our utmost scorn and unworthy of even the slightest shred of mercy. So shall you be punished accordingly."

At that, the throng, as one, bared their teeth and snarled at the woman in a demonstration of pure, visceral hate that was startling, even after all I had witnessed that day.

"Your death alone will not suffice. You must suffer, in prolonged agony, to purify yourself of your transgressions and to sanctify us. Your pain will cleanse those you should have cherished. It will purge us of the stain that you have left on our lineage, on our health and on our *honour*."

He spat the last word and turned, with a dramatic flourish, to the guards. Then, he drew a filthy hand across his neck in exaggerated slow-motion and shouted, "Burn her!" The crowd quickly took up the chant, bleating on cue, and I saw one of the henchmen take hold of a chain, which had been hanging over the branch of the stripped tree, and advance towards the squirming woman, grinning evilly.

That was my cue for action and I sprinted, at full tilt, to the trapdoor concealing the route I had taken to reach the rooftop. I removed the large stone with the desperate strength of a man possessed and shimmied down the ladder as quickly as possible, ignoring the bumps and pains from my protesting knees and shins as I went.

The stairway was deserted and in darkness, so I fished the torch out of my backpack and turned it on. Presumably, all the surviving inhabitants were gathered in the square downstairs or had perhaps fled, the sane minority, at least. I had no time for my usual caution, nor even to hold my breath against the stench of human waste, as I bounded down the steps towards the ground floor, using the handrail to stop me from falling and kicking bags of refuse out of my way as I went.

I reached the foyer, which was, thankfully, unoccupied, in record time and paused, for a brief second, to catch my breath and assess my approach. I listened for danger but heard nothing, so I cautiously ventured out into the street, turning off my torch for increased discretion. Luckily, the area was also deserted and eerily quiet, apart from the faint chanting that I could hear from the other side of the building.

I stooped to pick up a large piece of concrete that I saw on the ground, weighing it in my hand as I wrapped my fingers around the smooth edges and coolly recalled how effective a similar implement had been last time. Clutching my improvised weapon tightly, I crept up to a covered walkway that provided access to the square, between two adjacent buildings.

I could hear loud screams now and the chanting had intensified. I feared I might be too late, already, so I pressed on hurriedly up the alley until I could make out the crowd ahead and silhouettes from the fire flickering on the walls.

Just then, a small figure detached itself from the shadows immediately behind me and moved towards the square:

towards me. I started with a jump before I realised that it was only a child. The youngster stopped when they eventually saw me, hesitated a brief second, then approached, with no fear, until I could see it was a boy of about eight. I attempted a smile with my eyes as I raised a finger to my masked lips, but he still spoke loudly, and genially, to me.

"I went for a pee. Did I miss anything?" he enquired. I just motioned again for silence. His gaze fell from my face to the stone clutched in my hand. "Who are you?" he asked, his tone changed and his voice raised.

"No one, shut up," I hissed, quietly but firmly. His young face instantly transformed, twisting into a mask of hatred and disgust at the sound of my accent.

"You're a *foreigner*," he half-shouted, half-spat. He backed off and opened his mouth to scream a warning.

I genuinely wish I could say that I weighed up the value of action versus inaction, the death of a damaged child versus the saving of an innocent soul but, to my shame, it was nothing but pure instinct and self-preservation that drove me from then on.

I sprang forward and clasped my free hand over the brat's mouth, hoping that would shut him up but the tiny fascist instead tried to bite my fingers and free himself. Without thinking, I rammed him backwards, slamming the rear of his head hard into the wall but, despite the loud crunch, he was only dazed for a millisecond and opened his mouth to scream again, this time with real fear in his eyes.

Instinctively, I swung the rock in my right hand around and caught him a vicious blow on the temple. I felt his skull crack and give beneath the weight of the impact and he crumpled at my feet, the cry for help stillborn on his lips.

I looked, aghast, at his tiny corpse in silent shock, but I had no time to reflect on what I had just done as screams, resonating from the sick ceremony, snapped me back to my reason for being there. I slid stealthily along the wall until I was under the arch that marked the entrance to the square, making sure that I was hidden in the shadows. I looked out at what was taking place and was stopped short by the sheer horror of what I was seeing.

The chain had been wrapped around the woman's chest and legs in a kind of searing harness, intended to support, but not kill, her. A stooge was holding the other end in gloved hands, using the trunk of the tree as a pulley to suspend her body over the raging fire, close enough for her to blister and burn, agonisingly, but preventing her from falling into the flames and thus dying quickly.

The poor lady writhed, in frantic spasms of pain, as her skin visibly peeled and liquified in the heat of the blaze, but her howls were strangely muted, even from only a short distance away. She opened her mouth and torrents of blood came gushing out, streaming down her chin and sizzling in the flames as she gargled an attempt at a cry. I realised then why she could not scream: her tongue had been cut out.

The woman scrabbled at the chain to try and haul herself out of the heat's devastating reach, but she could not hold on to it. Her feet and hands, too, had been severed and were now nothing but bloody stumps. As the full realisation of her inhumane torture hit me, I leaned against the wall and vomited violently but, even as I was being sick, I felt a cold, vengeful rage begin to build inside.

I wiped my mouth clean and gripped the dark-stained stone tightly in my hand, sizing up the distance to the brute holding the chain. It was not too far, maybe twenty metres or so and my arm was good. I let fly viciously, aiming at his laughing face but I was slightly off-target, the rock arcing low and instead hitting him firmly in the solar plexus.

The blow caught him completely by surprise and he clutched at his body, winded by the impact. As he winced, the chain whipped out of his hands and over the tree, dumping his mutilated victim deep into the raging flames; although that would not save the poor lady, it would be an infinitely quicker end than otherwise. It would be a mercy, given her injuries, and the best result I, or she, could have hoped for in the situation.

The chanting immediately stopped. Everyone was suddenly silent, looking around frantically, searching for the source of the attack but they could not see me, almost invisible, in the shadows. The demagogue stood alone, looking around worriedly and I took my chance, drawing my knife and throwing it, in one movement, at the murderous bastard.

The blade only just missed his body but nicked his bare arm viciously as it flew by, before clattering loudly to the ground. He grabbed his wound and cursed loudly in indignant rage. That broke the indecision of the crowd, as they now knew for sure which direction the attacks were coming from, even if they could not see the assailant.

Not for the first time that day, I turned to flee for my life as the acolytes poured, as one, towards my hiding place, baying for blood. As I reached the end of the alley, a sudden cascade of guttural, anguished howls told me that they had found their dead child.

I sprinted back out onto the deserted street and headed north, away from the station square and the chaos I had seen earlier; the last thing I needed now was to run into a mass of people. I had to be cautious. If I encountered any setback on my route, anything to slow me down at all, I would fall into the rabid clutches of The Mob.

I looked down at the street below my shoes as I ran. The night was very dark and I could not afford to stumble or trip for even a millisecond. I vaulted an overturned waste bin, lying in the middle of the road, and the terrifying clamour of The Mob behind lent extra speed to my feet as they hit the tarmac without slowing me down.

As I was running, I could not be sure, but it sounded as though I was putting distance between myself and my pursuers. As such, I started to relax a little but then I made a catastrophic error. Instead of staying on the main road, I turned into a side street, taking an unnecessary chance in an attempt to lose The Mob but I quickly realised that, for the second time in a matter of hours, I had foolishly run into a dead end. This time, no amount of bravery or play-acting would save me. I was cornered and massively outnumbered.

I slowed to a stop, panting heavily in the night air as I looked desperately around me. There were buildings on both sides, blocking me in with sheer, unscalable walls. At the end of the side street was a large iron fence, impeding my progress. I ran up to it and looked through, despondently, as I heard The Mob come to a halt behind me, momentarily unsure of which way I had taken. Then I saw, through a crack between the metal sheets, the moon glinting off the rippling surface of the river, on the other side, and the shoots of an idea suddenly flowered in my mind.

I quickly tore off my shoes and socks, to enable me to get some kind of a grip on the corrugated iron with my bare feet, then took a running jump and caught hold of the top of the fence with my hands. Mercifully, my feet were clammy and they found a purchase on the cool metal instead of just sliding off. I scrabbled my way, undignifiedly, to the summit and hoisted my legs over with all the zeal and intent of a primate escaping its enclosure.

As I hauled myself over and eyed the big drop to the ground, I heard, then saw, The Mob flood into the alley behind. It screamed as it saw me and a hail of stones instantly flew in my direction, just as I landed on the other side of the fence. Most of the projectiles merely clattered deafeningly off the iron but a small rock sailed high, up and over the barrier, and caught me painfully on the side of the forehead.

I had no time to even wince, however, and I raced to the water's edge and dived headlong into the murky currents, taking a deep breath and praying that it was deep enough as I did so. To my immense relief, it was. Staying submerged, I aimed with powerful strokes for the middle of the river and surfaced noisily to attract the attention of my pursuers, who were now pounding and kicking on the fence behind me, with the obligatory mindless howling, of course.

I made a show of splashing around and slipped under the water, gasping for air and screaming loudly for help, just as the corrugated iron was brought crashing down. The first few constituent members of The Mob pointed and cheered triumphantly as they saw me 'drowning' in the river. They immediately began to shout abuse and jeer cruelly at my imminent end. Then, a fresh wave of rocks and assorted debris flew my way and splashed into the depths around me, though thankfully missing their mark.

I feigned receiving a hit, clutching my head in simulated pain and slipping under the water as if stunned. Once fully out of sight, I did an about turn and set off towards the opposite side, with powerful strokes of my arms, remaining hidden beneath the surface.

Eventually, after what seemed like an age and with my lungs almost bursting, I felt my fingers brush the bottom of the river as it climbed to meet the bank and I knew I'd made it. I rolled onto my back, still submerged, allowing only my face to break the surface to refill my screaming lungs, as I carefully looked around me.

On my immediate right was what looked like a small, wooden rowing boat, moored at the river's edge. I sculled ever so softly towards it through the water, without making a ripple or sound, until I was safely on the other side of the vessel, between it and the land, and out of sight of my pursuers on the opposite shore.

In a stroke of luck, the riverbank nearest me was overgrown and thick with vegetation: the perfect place to hide. More importantly, it was also deserted. I slid out of the water on my stomach, pulling myself onto dry land with my hands and staying low, staying out of sight.

I was shivering, a little, in the chill night air but I could not risk changing my clothes. My backpack was sodden at any rate, so the only thing to do was just ignore the feeling as best I could. At least my clothes would no longer be drenched in sweat, I thought, though I dreaded to think what they'd smell of after my unscripted dip in the river.

I pulled myself laboriously through the grass and weeds on my forelimbs, like one of our earliest terrestrial ancestors, ignoring the gash on my forehead that was now throbbing, insistently, after my impromptu swim. I worried for a second that it might get infected but then I reminded myself that I would be lucky to live long enough for that to become a problem, so I ignored it.

I looked cautiously back to the other bank to check the situation. The Mob had begun to disperse, apart from a few diehards that were standing at the river's edge, barking orders at a couple of men in the water. They were splashing around noisily, trying to find me, either to verify that I was dead or to finish me off if I wasn't. Judging by the words they were using to describe yours truly, they certainly were not looking to give first aid.

I lay completely still, concealed in the foliage, for what felt like an eternity, watching the murderous scumbags gradually give up, one by one, until they had all crawled away, either back to their lairs or off in search of other, more visible, victims.

I idly wondered where their leader was now and severely regretted not killing him with the knife I had thrown. I consoled myself, however, with the knowledge that he would be dead soon enough anyway: the virus spared none of its victims.

When the area was eventually clear of all danger, I sat up and pondered on my options. Immediately, I realised, yet again, how very limited they were. I looked at the riverbank above me and briefly considered climbing it, but God only knew what was on the other side, what horrors there awaited, and I did not care to find out.

My thoughts turned to the old rowing boat, its mooring rope straining ceaselessly against the steady current seeking to wash it away, downriver, down to the sea. Then, I had a brainwave: that battered little wooden vessel was my way out of the cursed metropolis.

I looked furtively in both directions and found that the river was now completely deserted, nobody on or even near it. The water's current would carry me out of the city, with little effort required on my part, and the darkness would mask my passing to all but the most watchful. If I kept low enough to the floor, even if I were spotted, all anyone would see was an old, brown boat that had broken its mooring, drifting aimlessly downstream to its eventual doom.

The new-found direction and positivity instantly lifted my spirits and I rose purposefully to my feet. I then immediately cursed myself for having thrown away my knife earlier.

The rope that moored the boat to the bank was attached and locked to a huge, solid iron peg, which was driven deep into the muddy grass at the river's edge. Using a nearby stick I managed to, after about ten minutes of painstaking digging, work the spike out of the ground. I tossed it and the rope into the craft triumphantly, then jumped in myself, using the crumbling oar I found inside to push myself clear of the land and into deeper water. I was away.

The decrepit vessel picked up speed as I paddled into the middle of the river, where the current was strongest, and a sudden memory flashed into my mind. I thought of an old ship, a ruined, rusty cargo vessel, run aground by the coast, that I'd taken a picture of on a holiday, many years ago. I had no idea if it would even still be there but it seemed like a good enough plan to try and find it. I felt a spark of hope flicker in my soul again at the idea.

Suddenly, I had a destination to aim for and a way of getting there. I was no longer merely running away, running for my life. Now, I was going *somewhere*. The thought improved my mood immeasurably and I allowed myself a little smile of contentment, for the first time in many hours, as I slipped steadily and silently downriver.

Out of the city.